OPHELIA'S
WORLD

OPHELIA'S
WORLD

—— or ——

The Memoirs of a Parisian Shop Girl

by Michele Durkson Clise

Clarkson N. Potter, Inc./Publishers

DISTRIBUTED BY CROWN

PUBLISHERS, INC., NEW YORK

Books by Michele Durkson Clise

My Circle of Bears
Ophelia's World

Published by Clarkson N. Potter, Inc., One Park Avenue,
New York, New York 10016, and simultaneously in Canada
by General Publishing Company Limited

Manufactured in Japan

LIBRARY OF CONGRESS CATALOGING IN
PUBLICATION DATA

Clise, Michele Durkson.
    Ophelia's world, or, The memoirs of a Parisian shop girl.

    I. Title.   II. Title: Ophelia's world.
PS3553.L56706   1984   813'.54.   83-24483
ISBN 0-517-55048-2

Designed by Tim Girvin Design, Inc.
10 9 8 7 6 5 4 3 2 1
First Edition

Frontis: OPHELIA B. CLISE

❧

TO THE MEMORY OF
MARGARETE STEIFF

january

OPHELIA B. CLISE

SCHNUFFY WITH M. RITZ

J A N U A R Y

JANUARY 1   The time has come to begin my journal of the life and times of the Bazaar des Bears, which Zenobia Onassis, my partner, says is in a shambles and which Clarence, my handsome, distinguished, dear good friend, says, shambles or not, is famous in all of Paris and deserves a history; and so, for accounting or for credit, the history begins.

The shop is closed today, the first day of the new year, and stands darkened, just a street away from our apartment, with its rose silk curtains drawn and its window empty, while M. Ritz, the watchful mouse, guards the door; we have had thefts, or anyway mysterious losses, in the last few months. But some of the shop's friends and mine are here with me in our *chambres des bonnes*, the converted servants' quarters where we live, and I will introduce them to the reader before the tale of the Bazaar des Bears gets underway.

I am Ophelia B. Clise. I first opened my shop three years ago when I returned to Paris, the city of my birth, from family travels around the world. My father was a diplomatic bear, stationed in Tibet, Malay, Kazakhstan, and now, alas, in Alaska, where my mother lives and shivers with him, wrapped in fur scarves and muffs. Together she and I collected cottons, silk, cloves, and dyes in the local markets of the East; we served French delicacies to the inhabitants, my father's guests. I returned to Paris to study roots and herbs; my father wanted me to be a nurse. But I kept around me all my mother's and my treasures— silver flutes, lace veils, chocolates, teas,

and sachets. My little room at school was so crowded that M. Ritz, who kept me company then, was sometimes lost for days. My parents began to send me bright feathers and jams from Alaska. It was then I made my plans to open a shop.

I met Zenobia at the University of Paris, in a class I wandered into by mistake—Varieties of Orange Blossoms. She was learning flower farming and medieval economic methods, and I liked her very much; after class she explained all the ancient trade routes of two hundred known kinds of nectars in crisp and fluid French. Zenobia is an American of Greek parentage, distantly related to the shipping family, and she understands accounting, which I certainly do not. We became business partners. Zenobia keeps the books, and she and Ricky Jaune, our concierge at the shop, and Clarence, who just this morning handed me a pretty little emerald ring, a New Year's present, and Heidi von Rosa and her friend, Clafouti, both of them collectors who help us with the shop in every way, all live together in seven charming "mansard" rooms atop a *hôtel particulier*, a nice old private townhouse owned by an elderly count and countess, on the rue de Varenne. We have a long, clear view of the roofs of Paris, including the gabled rooftop of the building on the nearby rue du Bac, where my shop, the Bazaar des Bears, is located.

Just now I hear a shout from Clarence, who is cleaning up the cups and bowls from the New Year's Eve celebration we gave for all our friends last night. "Here are *five* untouched plates of chocolate truffles underneath Clafouti's bed," he calls. Earlier he put away a chocolate cake with just one slice removed. He says we served too much. I like to quote Saint Bearnadelle, who said, *"D'avantage est rarement suffisant"* ("More is rarely enough"), but Clarence has good sense. Last night Schnuffy, who promised to begin to pose in the shop window tomorrow for the January display, ate a whole chocolate mousse with his paw, alone in a corner of the salon—I saw him—and limped wearily out the door at 3:00 A.M., a lesser bear.

> *"D'avantage est rarement suffisant."*
> (More is rarely enough)
> —Ophelia B. Clise

JANUARY 3   Yesterday Zenobia began to take an accounting of the contents of the entire shop—placing ribbons here, shawls and linens there, boxes with buttons and boxes with coins, Limoges cups, and tottering piles of annotated manuscripts on the tables and floor. She was dressed in an Edwardian brown corduroy suit

and kid gloves for this task, with a pencil tucked behind each ear. This morning she wore goggles! There is no dust in the shop, as Zenobia knows; Ricky Jaune dusts every day with as much concentration as Madame Defarge's when she knitted (although, of course, for kinder reasons), but I did not stop to point this out to her, because sometimes I think she misses floriculture and she may have been hoping to flush out a few of last summer's bees.

While Zenobia was launching her inventory and I was hanging the last strings of crystal beads in the window, Schnuffy came in, late and looking nervous. He was dressed for the window and climbed in, trying out his pose. I padded into our little well-stocked back room to look for a paper fan I remembered having seen, cut like snowflakes and perfect for a corner backdrop; and then I heard a whoosh and muffled crash of dried flowers, lace, and crystal falling into a delicate heap. The window! Had M. Ritz startled Schnuffy? I had not seen M. Ritz today. I rushed to the front of the shop, and when I got there Schnuffy was alone, looking left and right around him, appearing bewildered and sitting slumped over. "Chocolate nerves," he said. "That was a wonderful mousse Heidi and Clafouti made on New Year's Eve!" And then he blushed.

This morning Schnuffy has brought a telescope and astronomy books to look at while he poses, but he still jumps about and jangles the ice crystals in the window. I hear them tinkling from my desk. It seems strange that Schnuffy, a quiet, even scholarly bear, has of late become so unsettled and unsettling.

"...a marriage est l'amenient suffisant."

(More is rarely enough.) —Ophelia B Clise

1173 PARIS. — La Madeleine. — LL.

IN CELEBRATION OF SNOW
OPHELIA B. CLISE
INVITES YOU TO THE WONDER
OF A CHOCOLATE PARTY
—
SUNDAY EVENING
7 O'CLOCK

OPHELIA'S DESK FOR JANUARY

OPHELIA AND HER MENAGE

"Chocolate nerves," two days after our party? I have known Schnuffy for a long time, as long, almost, as I've known most of my friends: he helped me find the shop and move in the heavy armoires and tables. Shy and slow then, he was a funny sort of odd *déménageur*, or porter, trying to become an astronaut. I think I was his only paying job. He has a regal bearing and a miraculous and notable collection of vests. It took me many months to talk him into showing them in the window. But he seems to have some sort of nervous twitch—I hear a thumping and a little crash—what a mysterious affliction!

JANUARY 5   In spite of everything, the window is beautiful. The beds of sugar and the crystal ice drops capture the winter-white light of the Paris afternoon. When bears pass by on their way to the Italian embassy around the corner, all heads turn. Heidi von Rosa has asked permission to take a photograph. Everyone is wishing for snow.

JANUARY 6   *La Fête des Rois!* At sundown my dear Clarence comes into the shop with a *galette*, the traditional flat cake, and six bottles of Normandy sparkling *cidre* to celebrate the arrival of the three kings in Bethlehem two thousand years ago. Zenobia dispatches Ricky Jaune to find a crown, and she brings out an extra chair for the Pauper. Epiphany or not, her face is stern: her inventory taking is being interrupted and soon her mounds of goods will have to be pushed aside. Dear, dutiful Zenobia! Schnuffy climbs in from the window. He takes a seat quietly— morosely?—in a corner. Heidi and Clafouti trail in, wearing capes, and Mona Lisa, a ragpicker who often brings shoe buckles and scraps of Irish lace into the shop to sell, knocks and enters by Clarence's invitation. He has run into her on the boulevard St.-Germain, he says, waving a paw at her. For a moment everyone gathers around and admires the little green ring that Clarence gave me; I say, "It is a friendship ring. Clarence and I have been best friends for four years now!" In a nice, low voice, Clarence starts to say, "It is more than that, Ophelia," but the bell tinkles and Ricky returns with the crown. Soon the cake is cut. Ricky receives the slice with the bean in it, and he is crowned king. Gallantly he turns to Mona Lisa and asks her to become his queen. We cry out, "*Un discours! Un discours!*" and Mona Lisa rises and stammers, "I am very happy to be here this afternoon." And so, I think, are we all.

JANUARY 12   Ricky Jaune has had to replace two-thirds of the sugar in the window.

It has disappeared. I write this down for Zenobia's sake, because she says I am to keep a *record* of the shop. Three strangers came this morning; one bought an ivory honey caddy. Where has the sugar gone?

JANUARY 14   Little M. Ritz came carrying some papers to me in his teeth today. He found them in the window. One of them looks like Schnuffy's passport; the other has some printing on it about learning Japanese. I put them on my desk as a reminder to give them back to Schnuffy. They become buried in a snowfall of other papers right away. I ask M. Ritz to carry them back to the window and should remember to ask Schnuffy if he's going to take a trip. I forget.

JANUARY 15   The sugar beads have disappeared *again*. M. Ritz is nowhere to be seen. Are cats to blame? One of M. Ritz's jobs is to watch out for stray cats that roam around the neighborhood making mischief, and though I haven't seen any, I think it must be cats who took the sugar. Yes, it must be cats!

FIRST LESSONS
IN BEEKEEPING

C. P. DADANT

ZENOBIA ONASSIS

RICKY JAUNE AND M. RITZ

JANUARY 17   I waited up for Clarence tonight; he came home late, flushed deep brown with the pleasure of a purchase he had made—an "underground spy camera," he said, holding it up proudly. It was small, flat, and black and is supposed to take very detailed pictures. Clarence writes for newspapers about restaurants and food, under the *nom de plume* "Les Comestibles"; and many of the chefs, saucemakers, maîtres d', and diners in and out of Paris would like to find out who he is. He felt that a large camera sooner or later would give him away. Heidi, Clafouti, and I struck poses while he practiced, holding the camera like a palmful of hidden hazelnuts, and talked about the weather having delayed the pruning of the grapevines in the Loire.

Finally I got him alone.

"Clarence, can you come to the shop tomorrow afternoon?" I asked.

"No," he said. "There's a new *lumpia goreng* stand opening in Montmartre and I want to cover it, and on Friday I have to visit a tea shop in Montrouge."

"Oh. Can you come on Monday? I promise I'll only need you for a little while—I mean, I'll need your camera. Does it have an automatic timer? This is important to *Zenobia*," I said. Clarence sometimes thinks I'm a little whimsical, especially when he's busy.

Clarence, impressed, agreed.

JANUARY 20   The sky is a deep and stormy gray this morning, and Clarence says that snow is on the way. He's rarely wrong, my friend, Swiss-accurate Clarence. And so, before he pulls his galoshes over his paws and leaves for his office, we plan a party to celebrate the first snowfall of the year. We write out the guest list: the count and countess, whose house we live in, and their houseguest, Jean de Noël, an investment-banker bear who's always dressed as if he had an appointment with the minister of finance—that is if he still is with them in the apartments below our own; our friend Camille, who has been gloomy this fall and winter because she has had no parts to dance in the Ballet Ours; Albert and Anemone, two distinguished émigré acquaintances of ours, who came to Paris after Albert gave up his claim to the throne at New Forest to marry for ideal and, lately, threadbare love; Schnuffy, Heidi, and Clafouti, Ricky Jaune, and a few officials from the Italian embassy nearby.

As I am writing down Zenobia's name, she steps in from her boudoir, fully dressed, wearing a slicker and unfurling an umbrella. "A snow party?" she asks. "It's a lovely idea. I admit I like snow myself. But please, Ophelia, don't invite Conrad. And don't ask that fidgety bear Schnuffy either. So far, I must say, I have discovered *five* enameled berry jars and an entire packing case of English primrose honey to be missing from the shop, and the inventory isn't even half completed. I don't want to point a finger yet, but allow me to have my misgivings."

Of *course* I will invite Schnuffy. How preposterous! And Conrad? I haven't seen Conrad, an irregular visitor to the shop and a bit of a *roué*, for a month; I think he's out of town. But if he's here, I think we should invite him. I glance at Clarence, who is looking thoughtful. *Cats*, I think. It's cats. Neither Clarence nor I mention his camera to Zenobia. There will be time for that after the snow.

JANUARY 24   The snow has fallen for three days. I left the shop with Clarence at lunchtime to walk in the cloud-white gardens of the Tuileries. When I saw the paler white of snowdrops poking up beneath the benches and in the barer ground around the crusted lilacs, I thought: spring flowers—if I count them will they predict that I'll find love? I looked at my little ring. What does Clarence mean to me?

Our party is over and it was a great success. We danced while snow fell through the lighted Paris streets. We ate: *oeufs à la neige*, white-chocolate ravioli with hazelnut filling, chocolate-dipped profiteroles, and a chocolate Bavarian crème for energy. Albert and Anemone brought a special English tea with lavender, and I brought out some apple-blossom honey. As I watched the bears dash between the samovar and the bowl of hot chocolate on a side table, I whispered to Anemone, *"D'avantage est rarement suffisant,"* and we smiled.

Then, in the midst of dancing, a liveried messenger listed in with a huge armload of white lilacs and fumbled for the card, which was addressed to me. The dancing stopped for a moment. The room was quiet. I glanced at Clarence, who smiled—distractedly, I realized afterward; but at the time his smile seemed full of messages and my heart gave a little leap. I opened the card, which read: "From Jean de Noël, with terrible regrets that he is unable to attend, and profoundest compliments to the beautiful Ophelia." It was posted from the United States. I had no time to find a vase, and so I put the lilacs in the bathtub. Jean de Noël, as the countess and count have told us, loves a grand gesture. The scent of spring filled our rooms this morning, but for just a moment, when I glanced across the breakfast table at Clarence, munching on his shredded wheat, the scent seemed melancholy. Then it seemed— like spring.

JANUARY 28   I showed all our beautiful Spanish shawls to two fashionable Right Bank bears. They took the four best ones away with them, and were happy.

JANUARY 29   A mysterious calling card was stuck in the shop door this morning when Ricky and I arrived—from one Brady Boeing. So far no Brady Boeing has showed up, but Albert phoned to say that he and Anemone will be *very* pleased to appear in the window in February—does the shop have heat? Poor dears! They must wait until the first day of the second week to begin, when their best ruffs will have been dry-cleaned.

JANUARY 31   Schnuffy laughs and rubs his paws together when I ask him, "Could you, by any chance, Schnuffy, spend another week . . .?" and then tries to look sober, nods, and scuttles back into the window. Rustle. Thump. *Crash!*

February

February 3

Sent pattern for container
to hold truffles to Atelin
des Bears. They will
make the corners of
pink and blue striped
paper similar to the one
I purchased at a Con-
fiserie in Paris.

February 5

Order chorola
from the B
specify da

February 6.
My dreams were
filled with visions
of bees in a very
beautiful garden.
I could hear the
sounds of summer
and I longed to
be in France.
Zenobias interpret-
ation of this is that
I know she is
First Lessons

OPHELIA'S DESK

F E B R U A R Y

FEBRUARY 7   Before dawn this morning, while the household slept, Clarence and I slipped around the corner to the rue du Bac and hung his little camera from a low limb of the *marronnier d' Inde* tree that stands across the sidewalk from the shop. We camouflaged it with brown leaves and twigs and ran a string from its little shutter button down the tree trunk, along the cracks in the sidewalk, through the window of the shop and tied it to the most tempting string of sugar pearls. When we had done all this, we crouched down behind the tree, hoping to be rewarded by the sight of some of the tumbledown neighborhood cats creeping toward the window and tripping off the camera with their claws. Just then, however, we heard the footfall and mordant whistling of M. Grandiose, the district *gendarme*, who was strolling along, beating the tree trunks with his baton. This brought Clarence and me quickly to our feet. The *agent de police* cocked a lavish eyebrow and said, "*Bonjour*, Mademoiselle Clise and monsieur. A charming day to dig for worms, is it not? A shame that the ground appears to be frozen, like wood or stone." With that he frowned and gave the chestnut tree a *thwap* for authoritative emphasis. Clarence and I winked at each other and Clarence left for work.

And so, by the very early hour of nine o'clock, when Zenobia and Ricky Jaune tinkled in together, I had already written out orders for stocks of tea, ribbon, glass buttons, chocolate bonbons, cinnamon, and motley other items that we always need. Zenobia puffed up a little with surprised approval. By the time Schnuffy arrived—and when had Schnuffy grown so stout? I wondered; two buttons on his vest were popped! I'd begun the long, pleasant task of folding red-paper roses for the Saint Valentine's Day window display. I kept my expectant expression hidden beneath my lowered toque, but at noon, when Schnuffy left the window for an hour, I listened above the clattering of teaspoons being sorted by Zenobia for any sign—a feline gasp, a panicked scampering—that the camera had been tripped and the culprits dispatched.

It was teatime before I admitted to myself that the cats might not come today and tied my scarf about my throat and went out to have some hot apricot soup and honey rolls for lunch; by then I was very hungry. Ricky Jaune was gossiping with two local teenaged pinball-playing bears, new friends of his whom he's been seeing a lot of lately, as I slipped out the door; and at that very moment, M. Ritz darted from around the corner, tore between my paws, and leaped into the cracked shop door before it settled closed. I started and leaned against the window to regain my balance, and *pop! flash! sizzle!* went Clarence's camera; and my scarf and toque, new walking suit, and astonished eyes and mouth, as I imagined them, were captured by the box.

I went and had some soup, but that was not the end of the day's adventures. As I approached the shop again the sun was going down, and I could just discern a tiny, dark form pacing back and forth a few yards from the window. When it saw me, it said, *"Psssst!"* and I recognized M. Ritz. He began to make indicative forward movements with his little head and ears, and I followed him around another corner, onto the rue du Cherche-Midi and into a diminutive cheese shop there that I had never seen before. M. Ritz gestured for me to sit, and I sat with care on a tottering mouse-sized stool. With trembling paws M. Ritz produced a folded piece of paper. I smoothed its folds and read:

> *Dear M. Ritz,*
>
> *Thank you very much for keeping our appointment today. What I have to tell you isn't easy. By now Ophelia and you know that someone has been eating sugar from the window. M. Ritz, that someone is me, Schnuffy! I'm very sorry—and I know that I've betrayed a trust. But something has happened to me lately; over the last few months I have come to want sugar all the time. I think it began on that picnic near Dijon in September, when Ophelia baked a cake in the shape and size of the Hôtel Aubriont. It grew worse at Christmastime, when Clarence kept taking us all for walks past Lenôtres. Now a rosy haze surrounds me whenever I see sugar anywhere; in a few hours it turns to a black fog and I have to start to eat again.*
>
> *I don't know what else to do about this, so I've booked passage on a freighter that sails from Marseilles for Japan tonight—the Kabuki Maru. I've heard that sugar hasn't been discovered in Japan yet; and I hope to give it up there and to concentrate on learning sumi, practicing aikido, and*

walking quietly among the worn, round hills, looking at the stars. Please tell Ophelia that I am her friend, that I am sorry, and that I will write to her just as soon as I am,
> *A reformed bear,*
> *Love,*
> *Schnuffy*

Poor Schnuffy! We should have suspected his affliction sooner! Then M. Ritz plucked the paper from my paw, jostled a pencil from the little satchel he was carrying, and wrote: "I was late meeting Schnuffy this afternoon. I'm sorry if I knocked you down." I patted M. Ritz's head a little absentmindedly and then rose to go consult with Clarence.

FEBRUARY 11   Zenobia and our local postman, an elderly bear whose small, neat form Zenobia has always liked, are having a morning cup of chocolate together as I sort through the mail: bills, an order from Nantes, a tradesman's circular, and four letters. I open the first of these. It is from Dr. Ernest Churchill, announcing a visit to Paris in March and April and expressing an interest in appearing in the window, which he thinks will be a good observation post for spying out Parisian butterflies. In addition to being a decorated minister of the queen of England, a scholar, a soldier, and a professional criminologist, Dr. Churchill is an accomplished lepidopterist. Two years ago, Zenobia and I met him walking in the woods near Bath; we were pretending to ourselves to be the Misses Bennet of *Pride and Prejudice*, which we were reading aloud to each other, and Dr. Churchill,

HEIDI VON ROSA AND CLAFOUTI

OPHELIA WITH FEATHERS

with his net, stumbled into us and invited us to tea. He became our own Colonel Fitzwilliam, and we've always wanted him to pay a visit.

The second letter—a photograph with just a note—makes me a little sad. It is from Schnuffy, mailed from aboard the *Kabuki Maru* somewhere in the Mediterranean near Egypt. I am so glad to hear from him! The note says: Perhaps a rice diet is the answer. I miss you. Do you forgive me? Love, Schnuffy. P.S.: I didn't take the missing berry jars and honey I heard Zenobia talk about. I promise!"

Of course he didn't—Clarence and I, while we were huddling and brooding together and exclaiming over the misfortunes of poor Schnuffy, agreed about that right away. We agreed too that we will miss him—his murmured explanations of astronomy, his talk of quarks named Strangeness, Spin, and Charm, his penciled sketches of all of us in spaceships—until he returns to us again.

The third envelope contains a pretty Saint Valentine's Day card from Clarence; the fourth, a note, says that Jean de Noël will soon be back in Paris, and might he call on me in the shop some afternoon? I answer, "Yes, we'll be delighted," and belatedly thank him for the lilacs he sent; write a few affectionate and consoling lines to Schnuffy; and then turn my attention back to the Saint Valentine's Day window, where Albert and Anemone are just giving a lunchtime pawful of hay to their horse, who is posing with them.

FEBRUARY 14　　This evening everyone comes in evening dress and gathers around Albert and Anemone in the window. I am

wearing red velvet and lace. Zenobia wears a white tea gown and carries bunches of carnations and Queen Anne's lace to a table in the center of the room, while Clarence, in a dinner jacket and workman's gloves, follows with the centerpiece of pink chocolate hearts and kisses in a basket made of chocolate. Heidi, Clafouti, and their friends, some painters from the *école*, erect a canvas on an easel and begin, by turns, to paint a depiction of true love: a couple in a bower, surrounded by birds and bees and fruit. It looks a lot like a Dante Gabriel Rossetti, except that every living thing seems to be female—even the birds and bees wear little bonnets. Now that I think about it, this is true of all of Heidi's and Clafouti's friends' paintings. It may be a new school.

FEBRUARY 22 Zenobia and I make an appointment to have dinner together by ourselves next week. It is time we talk about Schnuffy and the sugar, and I hear from her how her inventory goes and whether she has found any other things to be missing or awry. Zenobia has more and more acquired the air of a dedicated secret agent on campaign. Last week when I tried to enter the back room to fetch some ribbon for a waiting customer, the closed door behaved just like a living thing: it yielded when I tugged, as doors most often do, but then snapped resolutely closed again, breathing alarmedly and sounding just like Zenobia. I'm sure it was Zenobia, acting very oddly. I went and looked for other ribbon beneath the counter, and I found it, but I think it's time for us to have a reassuring talk. Our mysteries aren't that serious!

FEBRUARY 29 Leap year day. I can see from my bedroom window that the little climbing rose sheltered by the back door of the house is in ivory bud. The doorbell rings, and a messenger delivers a box of chocolates into my paws. They are from "Le Dilettante," says the card; they have been sent from "Seattle." What a beautiful tinkling ring that word Seattle has! It reminds me of the frozen rivers of the north my mother describes for me in her letters, overhung with ice crystals and filled with little fish. Perhaps I shall add the word Seattle to my card. The chocolates are from Jean de Noël, and they are the most delicious chocolates I've ever eaten in my life.

Jean de Noël
MONTE CARLO
Principauté de Monaco

March

AUNT VITA

DR. CHURCHILL

M   A   R   C   H

MARCH 2   On a bright, beautiful springlike morning there are six or eight browsers in the Bazaar des Bears inspecting sun-washed merchandise: a maiden aunt and her nephew admiring a leather case fitted with old drafting tools; a young *matron* at a mirror holding a black-feathered cloche to her head, tilted. A happy hum of chatter fills the air. I sit at my desk to write a note of thanks to Jean de Noël for the chocolates, before the post. Might we order other boxes from Seattle? I ask him. And where *is* Seattle? The bell above the glass door tinkles. It is Mona Lisa, threading her way through the band of customers, who step aside a little as she passes. Mona totters and looks shy; she is wearing shoes of different heights and a dress that trails along the floor. When she reaches my desk, she holds out a pair of eighteenth-century lace gloves to me and smiles toward the center of the room, as though a banquet might be laid there or a childhood friend has suddenly appeared. I know very little about Mona Lisa—only that she lives somewhere near the rue du Faubourg St.-Antoine, where hundreds of rooms are for rent in hundreds of old houses, and that she loves to hunt through the street for treasures. *"Bonjour,* Mona," I say gently, taking the gloves from her. *"Tout va bien?* It is a beautiful day."

"Yes," she says, "thank you," and strays toward a set of silver chimes beside my desk, which she touches and sets ringing. Her smile darkens for a moment. "I saw Conrad," she says. She lowers her voice and adds, "These gloves are his."

"And he gave them to you as a gift?" Conrad collects gloves. I look at them and decide they will be beautiful with a little mending of one finger. They are intricate and made for a small and delicate paw, which Mona Lisa has. But Mona doesn't answer; instead she listens to the soft ringing of the tinkling chimes and looks frightened. I'm glad to know that Conrad is in Paris, and nearby— months ago he promised to appear in the April

YOUNG DR. CHURCHILL

window. Perhaps he has forgotten, but I have not.

I settle Mona in a chair and set about to make her some hot chamomile tea.

MARCH 4   Last night, as Zenobia and I were darkening the shop and about to go out in the rain for dinner, a wet, drab-blue–suited *agent des postes et telegraphe* rapped lightly at the door and handed Zenobia a telegram. It was from Dr. Churchill. "Arriving by boat train tomorrow evening," Zenobia read out. The message went on to say that Dr. Churchill had heard reports that flocks of rare butterflies—*Papilionidae*—were flying north toward Paris on their way to The Hague this week and that he wanted to take up his station in the window right away. This was decisive: There would not be time to mount a full-scale lepidopteran display, as we had wished. But what could we do instead?

Zenobia and I went to look for Ricky Jaune to advise and help us. When we found him, we all walked to the Café-Tabac, talking about the coming spring, developments in pinball, and finally the March window. Ricky Jaune was adamant that we make "crime and punishment" the window's theme, celebrating Dr. Churchill's interest in forensic psychology. By the time the three of us were seated for dinner, however, and dipping our spoons into some clear, tart, delicious aspic jelly, we had agreed that it would be easier and best to honor Dr. Churchill's military service to his queen. We had all the clippings, brochures, and snapshots he had sent us, and we knew what medals and decorations he had won. Even before dessert was served, Ricky Jaune rushed back to the shop to begin assembling mementos and *matériel*, and so Zenobia and I were left alone.

I began our appointed conversation about the shop. I told Zenobia about my suspicions of the cats and my misadventure with the "spy" camera, to make her laugh, and then read her Schnuffy's letter to M. Ritz. When I had finished, Zenobia said, "I thought as much," and went on.

"The sugar doesn't matter, Ophelia—you didn't have to keep it from me. I wasn't worried. Of course, first I thought that its disappearance might have something to do with the disappearance of other things—the set of Meissen dinnerware that wasn't in the back room, where it was supposed to be, last fall; the Charles V silver tea service we couldn't find on that day in November—remember?—when the countess sent her friend the marquise to look at it; and then the shipment of Keemun tea that just vanished at Christmastime, when so many bears were in and out. I think the case of honey and the enameled jars must have disappeared at the same time, although certain gaps in our receipt record—no, Ophelia, I'm not nagging you!—make it hard to tell."

Zenobia paused and noticed that the look on my face was not one of protest but of surprise. "Oh, yes," she said, "all those things are still missing, and for a while, when I noticed the sugar was disappearing too, I thought of Schnuffy. But the other foodstuffs—the honey and the tea—had disappeared in bulk—cases of them!—and nothing large or valuable was missing from the shop while he was in the window. Jittery or not, I don't believe that he's our thief."

OPHELIA'S DESK FOR MARCH

I had never put all these disappearances together in this way before. I thought we had misplaced some things—the silver set, for instance. I know we are disorganized, but I can't believe we're being robbed. "Who is it, Zenobia?" I asked. "Do you really think we have a thief?"

"I don't know, Ophelia. I think we must have one, but I don't know who it could be. My misgivings . . . they're just vague and indistinct doubts. I haven't finished the inventory yet, but when I do I think we ought to hold a meeting of the bears. In the meantime, let us warn M. Ritz."

We finished our soufflé and walked home together, lost in thought.

MARCH 5   Dr. Churchill has arrived and is installed, a triumph! He is so stout and remarkable looking among the window ribbons and the photographs that Right Bank bears have come in twos and threes to quiz us slyly about who he is. Ricky Jaune assembled everything, and the two of them—Ricky and the Doctor—already are fast friends. Yesterday they debated happily the value of new speech pattern analysis for identifying criminals, of which Ricky said disdainfully, M. Grandiose and even the *préfet de police* are unaware; and now Dr. Churchill is showing him the best way to bring a butterfly to bay. Ricky's "Ums" and "Ahs" make a pleasing counterpoint to Dr. Churchill's sanguine, rolling, English-sounding French. Each of them occasionally lifts his opera glasses to look for the migrant southern butterflies, which Dr. Churchill calculates will fly this way tomorrow or the next day. All of

us, Zenobia included, are very glad that he is here—bespectacled Fitzwilliam!

MARCH 10   The *Papilionidae* did arrive, and Ricky, Dr. Churchill, and even dear, proper Clarence, who was visiting the shop for tea, flew out into the street to net a few, causing

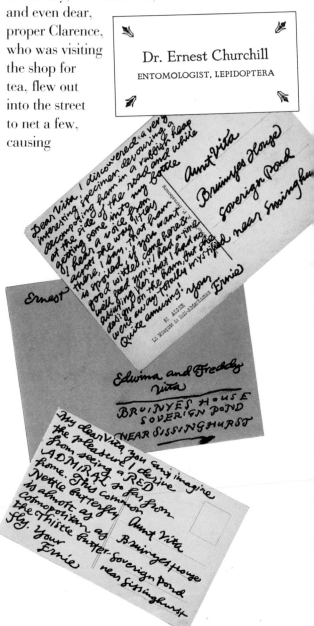

a bicycle accident, a small uproar, and the renewed attentions of M. Grandiose who tried and failed to disperse the butterflies with his baton; we soothed him with a piece of chocolate cake. As the bicyclers argued about right of way and Ricky chased a fugitive butterfly into the window, suddenly there appeared in the doorway, like a returning hero bearing gifts, Jean de Noël. He was small, handsome, and calm. He bowed to Clarence and Zenobia and then to Dr. Churchill. He kissed my paw and handed me another large, beautifully wrapped box of Dilettante chocolates, saying, "Since you approve of them, you shall have more. I have arranged for the American proprietor to open a second shop in Paris—six doors from your own. My compliments." He held my paw and said that he was hemmed in right now by business; soon he must leave Paris for Morocco. Was there anything that he might bring me from the colonies? He would stop and see me before he left, but would I have dinner with him after he returned, in May? I thought I heard a snort of derision from Clarence and Zenobia before I answered yes. Then Jean de Noël was gone again.

MARCH 18   "I have been thinking," says Dr. Churchill as he steps out of the window, "of my dear, unfortunate Aunt Vita. Poor bear will be ensconced—nay, really almost imprisoned—this August in our National Trust house in Kent, with only our butler and housekeeper, Freddie and Edwina, to keep her company. What would you think about inviting her here to Paris for September? The

change of air, the scenery, new acquaintances— especially you and Clarence and that bright boy Ricky Jaune—would do her so much good."

We issue an invitation for September right away.

MARCH 27   Conrad hasn't forgotten his offer to appear in the window in April, after all. When I return from the *marché* St.-Germain he is standing in the middle of the shop floor, paws behind his back, felt hat tipped toward his forehead, watching Zenobia sort through a drawerful of stamps with an air of wanting to talk but not being sure of what to say. Conrad is sometimes shy. He and *I* chatter—about the window and about Bern, where he has been touring with an opera company since January. He designed their sets. When I ask him about Mona Lisa's gloves, he looks uncomfortable. "I gave them to her from my collection," he says. "But she didn't want them. She stuffed them in an old brown bag. I know they were a little torn—I lent them to the opera company in Bern. . . ." This soon leads to the brighter subject of the Bern production of *Don Giovanni et Ours*, and leads Conrad to remember another reason why he's visited the shop: He has also designed the sets for *Madame Butterfly*, the opening production of the Parisian Opéra, and wants all of us to come to opening night in April as his guests. When he walks out onto the rue du Bac he is whistling softly, and I turn to unpacking the treasures I have found in the Clignancourt *marché aux puces*—including the handsomest crystal egg I have ever seen.

April

CONRAD WITH PRINCE ALBERT AND ANEMONE

APRIL 1   Conrad has been standing in the window for six hours now, posing as the king of Easter eggs—his own idea. Clarence and Dr. Churchill, both full of enthusiasm for the idea, helped Conrad put the finishing touches on his crown last night. Then Dr. Churchill rifled through the books he carries with him and supplied Conrad with a motto for his reign: "I prefer to be where there is no jostling."

I prefer to be where there is no jostling.
Marcel Proust

                                         supposedly from Proust . . .
A la recherche du temps perdu.
Conrad liked the quote so much he patted Dr. Churchill on the back and said it would be his motto for all time.

    The only one not delighted by Conrad's presence in the window this morning was Zenobia, who, I imagine, prefers to keep all outsiders—except customers, of course—out of the shop until our affairs have been straightened out. For some reason she especially disapproves of Conrad. Is this because of his reputation as a mild and charming rake? His longish hair? His clothing, which seems too richly cut for the wages of a part-time set designer? Whatever her objection to him, Conrad has detected it and seems to be trying very hard to win her over—asking Zenobia about her methods of bookkeeping, offering her chocolates, even trying to joke with her. She laughed a little at his jokes, and when he asked her to be his special companion at the opera on opening night, I actually thought I saw her blush. Since then—about an hour ago—there has been a marked quieting of the scratching of her pen on her logbooks, as she finishes the March accounts.

APRIL 3   Mona Lisa stood transfixed in the rain this afternoon, staring through the window at Conrad, and then disappeared into the mist, like a wraith, before I could invite her to come in. Later I caught a glimpse of her hunching like a gypsy under the *métro* pavilion at the corner of the street. The veil of her hat was pulled low, and she seemed to be reading but was really taking notes on the flyleaf of a book that said in large block letters LEARN TO THINK IN RUSSIAN. I was chasing a rail-thin German matron who had demanded we sell Conrad to her; she wanted him for the dining-table centerpiece of an Easter supper she was giving with two cardinals. She called M. Ritz a "nasty vermin" on her way out the door but had the bad luck to leave her packages behind, and M. Ritz refused to bring them to her, though he's much faster on his paws than I. I was out of breath by the time I returned to look for Mona Lisa. I thought I saw a disappearing trail of a print silk dress at the *métro* stairway, but Mona Lisa was gone again.

APRIL 6   As I was polishing the Clignancourt crystal egg this morning, getting ready to place it in a glass case with prisms and two wooden puppets, a ray of sunlight struck the egg and I noticed something unusual about it that was even lovelier than its shining surface and its rounded shape: a murky phosphorescence in its center, which seemed to shift in place and change in color, from coral to faded crimson. I carried the egg to Zenobia's desk to show it to her. Just then the bell tinkled, and I forgot the egg—I put it down to take the paw of Jean de Noël, who had come to say good-bye.

RICKY JAUNE

APRIL 8   What a fuss! The commercial attaché from the Italian embassy was here, dragging two crates of new espresso coffeepots behind him. He wanted us to put the clunky things in the window in May—for Italian import month. Zenobia told him absolutely no and dispatched him with a clatter.

APRIL 13   It is our night at the opera. We quit the shop early, leaving Ricky Jaune and his new young pinball-playing friends in charge, and walk in the Jardin du Luxembourg to see the jonquils reflecting the bright yellow of the afternoon spring sun before we separate to dress for dinner. Clarence and I, refreshed by walking, do not want to stop; arm in arm, our gaits well matched, we stroll along the quai Voltaire onto the upper rue du Bac to have some tea and cakes. Then, as we enter a tiny little tea shop on the rue de Verneuil, I remember: This is where Clarence and I first met, four years ago! Right away I see the dour visage of the *garçon* who menaced me in this very spot. And there, climbing over the brioches like a soldier on patrol, is probably a descendant of the self-same fly that I complained had dived into my sugared tea. The old waiter at first had denied this strenuously and actually blamed *me* for bringing flies into the *salon de thé*. Clarence stood up from a neighboring table and put the waiter in his place. He retreated and Clarence said to me in a low and comforting voice that I ought not let myself be taken advantage of. Then as he walked me back to my little room at school, I thought that he was awfully

CONRAD

MONA LISA

handsome and self-assured. A year later, when I met Zenobia and we made plans to open the Bazaar, we three moved in together. It took a little while before Clarence stopped watching over me like an older, protective brother; but sometimes he still does. I glance at him now to see whether he recalls this place, that time, the fragrant tea, the old *garçon*; but Clarence is absorbed in hefting and tasting his almond bread—professional business—and does not look up to see the waiter's crotchety glare or my musing.

When we return at six to the rue de Varenne

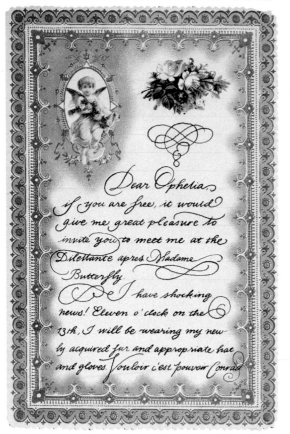

Dear Ophelia,

if you are free, it would give me great pleasure to invite you to meet me at the Dilettante apres Madame Butterfly.

I have shocking news! Eleven o'clock on the 13th, I will be wearing my newly acquired fur and appropriate hat and gloves. Vouloir c'est pouvoir Conrad

there is a note from Conrad waiting for me. He wants me to meet him at the newly opened Dilettante Chocolaterie after the performance; he has some "shocking" news to give me. Now what can this be? I have no time to wonder because Zenobia walks into the salon from her boudoir and dazzles my eyes: She has never looked so lovely as she does this evening in a dress of airy pale rose silk chiffon and a cape of deeper colored faille. I hurry to dress myself in an ivory satin dress I have borrowed from the shop, and then Zenobia and I each take one of Clarence's proffered arms and stride out into the evening to meet Conrad and Dr. Churchill, feeling gay and ornamental.

The opera is spirited and rousing; the sets and the old Opéra itself, with its red velvet curtains and its painted ceiling by Chagall, are lovely. At intermission we eat glazed mandarin-orange sections, and at the end of the performance we stand and applaud with all our might—Dr. Churchill most loudly of all. Conrad escorts Zenobia, who has really enjoyed the pure, sweet singing and the pageantry, backstage to meet Madame Butterfly. Dr. Churchill, Clarence, and I hail a taxi and go home, where I cast off my dress, change, and make a hasty exit for the Dilettante.

Le Dilettante Chocolaterie has turned out to be a charming toy-sized shop, redolent of citrus peel, peppermint, and chocolate. Conrad, still in evening dress, waits for me at one of two tiny wrought-iron tables. His paws are clasped tightly together, and lines of worry crease his face. When he sees me, though, he jumps up and tries to smile in a breezy, happy way. This fails, and he looks like a bear being brave while his tooth is extracted. "Ah, Ophelia," he says, seating himself again, "I'm so glad you could come, though it was silly of me to call you out. I don't have 'shocking news,' not really—I don't know why I said that. Isn't the Dilettante a fine addition to the street? Here, have a fondant. I'm just a little worried about a reduction of the sets for *Carmen with the Bear Chorale*, the next production after *Madame Butterfly.* It's not serious, really. Aren't these bonbons good? Why don't you take some home to Zenobia? She likes chocolates, doesn't she?"

"Certainly," I say, and think: You aren't telling me the truth, Conrad. You've changed your mind about whatever it is you wanted to say to me, and now you're trying to cover up. What was it? Why do you have that guilty look on your face? Conrad doesn't give me an opening to ask, and so I listen as he praises Zenobia's "solemn beauty," her fine mind, her excellent ear. He seems genuinely fond of her; *this* is not a pretense. I think that Zenobia is beginning to like him too. I start to tell him this, but Conrad does something extraordinary as I speak: He clutches his head in his gloved paws and moans; then he recovers himself and smiles that tortured smile again. Heavens! What is this all about? Is something really wrong?

Conrad walks me home, and he won't let me ask him any questions. Every time I do he starts singing "Un Bel Di" in a loud, high voice. Finally I go to bed and to sleep and for some reason dream of bears in paradise with

ZENOBIA WITH FRIEND

jonquils, well fed and well loved, every one.

APRIL 16   It was Bazaar des Bears week at the *Paris-Match* today. A photograph of Zenobia and Conrad, paw in paw, taken backstage at the opera chatting with Madame Butterfly, appeared in the pages of the magazine; Heidi and Clafouti were shown at a gallery opening; and Clarence, who is very much unnerved, was shown talking to a chef in the background of a photograph taken in the Tour d'Argent. "Anonymity is my stock-in-trade," he kept muttering this morning, although I do not think his anonymity has been much diminished; Dr. Churchill needed all the

Dear Ophelia,

If you are free, it would give me great pleasure to invite you to meet me at the Dilettante après Madame Butterfly.

But I have shocking news! Eleven o'clock on the 13th, I will be wearing my newly acquired fur and appropriate hat and gloves. Pouvoir c'est pouvoir

Conrad

POUDRE
ADHÉRENTE & INVISIBLE

NYMPHEA

LORENZY-PALANCA
PARIS

DOUBLE CEMENT PERI
DEDICATED TO & ACCEPTED BY THE
BARON VON HUMBOLDT

180B Jerkin

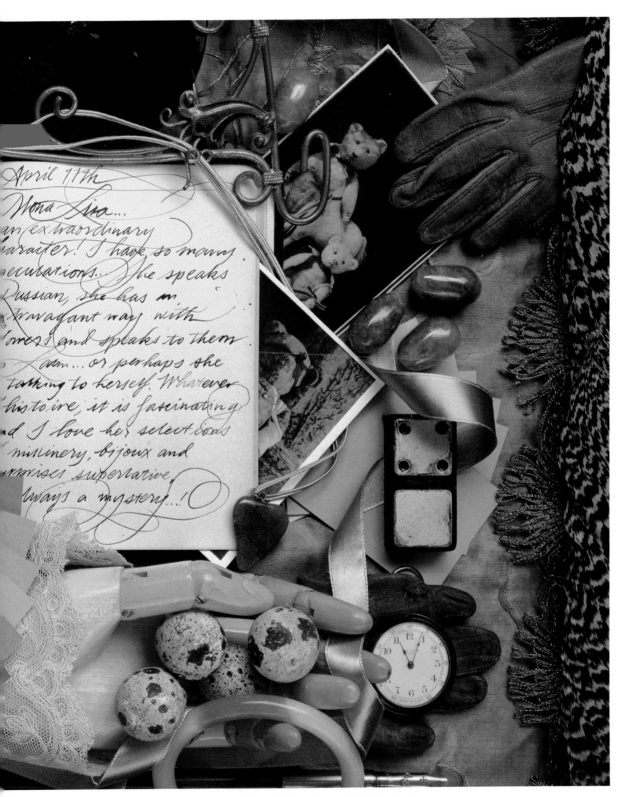

April 17th
Mona Lisa...
an extraordinary
character! I have so many
speculations... She speaks
Russian, she has an
extravagant way with
flowers and speaks to them
even... or perhaps she
talking to herself. Whatever
histoire, it is fascinating
and I love her; select bon
millinery, bijoux and
surprises superlative,
always a mystery...!

OPHELIA'S DESK FOR APRIL

power of his thick pince-nez to find him in the picture, and Dr. Churchill knows him very well.

APRIL 21   Marcello, the ambassador from Italy, was dispatched by his attaché to intervene with us about the espresso pots. This time we agree to display a few—if Marcello will appear with them in May. We drive a hard bargain. He concedes.

APRIL 23   Conrad has not been able to be in the window since our night at the Opéra. He says that preparing for *Carmen* is taking more time than he thought, but I am worried about him. M. Ritz is out chasing cats. Zenobia is quiet. I think she misses one of them, Conrad or M. Ritz.

APRIL 25   I am alone in the shop sorting invoices when Mona Lisa tiptoes in, slides from table to table, touching this and that, and tiptoes out again, never having said a word. She is a mystery! I didn't want to disturb her, because she is so shy and secretive—she once ran right out the shop door when Clarence boomed, "Well, and how are *you*, Mona Lisa?" from behind her. I wish she had asked me, though, for whatever she was looking for. The shop has never been so well organized in all its history. It is stocked, inventoried, and accounted for and we can lay our paws upon any scrap of ribbon, doll's slipper or darning needle at a moment's notice and without a search.

MARCELLO

Ambassador to Rome

Improvisations pianissimo

MARCELLO

ZENOBIA

APRIL 28 Oh-oh! Something has *really* gone wrong this time. Suddenly our happy family is full of confusion and downheartedness! Zenobia is crying in her room. Ricky Jaune has run *away*, and Dr. Churchill has run out to follow him. Clarence is questioning M. Ritz, who just strayed innocently in. The fact is that the crystal egg I found at Clignancourt and liked so much has vanished, disappeared without a trace, and Dr. Churchill says there is not a doubt that it has been stolen.

SCHNUFFY IN JAPAN

May

POPIE AND MARCELLO WITH M. RITZ

MAY 1   Well, it gives me pleasure to record that it is a sweet, fragrant first May morning, and the life of our shop and the hearts of its friends are a little bit more settled now, almost calm again. Ricky Jaune is standing by the door once more, watching the comings and goings in the street, although he has cried once or twice since Dr. Churchill brought him back. Zenobia too is quiet and pale. She has such an orderly, alert good mind that she cannot help but notice things that are amiss, especially when they're things she loves, and try to set them right; but none of us, least of all Zenobia, who is really sentimental about people, was ready for an outright theft under mysterious circumstances, almost before our very eyes, or for hearing our friends listed, even by another friend, as possible suspects. Dr. Churchill himself looked surprised by what occurred before he ran out the door to try to find poor, dashed Ricky Jaune.

That afternoon, Marcello, the Italian ambassador, had just ambled out after settling some little details about the May window when the bell above the door tinkled again, and Dr. Churchill bustled in with a large, dark, handsomely groomed stranger on his arm. They were talking excitedly together, and Zenobia and I and Ricky Jaune, who was filling in for Conrad in the window, and Clarence and the countess, who had stopped by, gathered round and were introduced to the stranger, I. G. Goods, an old friend of Dr. Churchill's visiting from London. Mr. Goods, Dr. Churchill told us, was a

scientific investigator and collector of antique "phenomena." He was eager to see my crystal egg that, from Dr. Churchill's description of it, he thought might be a rare and valuable egg lost from a London curiosity dealer's shop a hundred years ago. We hurried to get it for him. But where was it? I remembered setting it down on a table days before, on the morning of the day Jean de Noël sailed for Morocco (the touch of his paw on mine still lingered); but the egg was not there now. Had anybody seen it since? No one had. Mr. Goods looked upset; it could be *very* valuable, he said. Zenobia and Dr. Churchill took up the search in earnest then, pushing aside chests and boxes in the shop and the back room, but the only thing they found was one of Conrad's gloves beneath a table; the egg was nowhere to be found.

By this time Mona Lisa had tottered in, and Clarence was assisting in the hunt. When every corner had been searched, he was the first to speak. "Well, it will turn up," he said, encouragingly, putting his arm around my shoulder. But Dr. Churchill coughed and said, "I don't believe so, Clarence. In fact, I have no doubt at all that the crystal egg has been stolen."

A cry broke out, everyone beginning to exclaim, protest, and remember things— mostly irrelevant things, like the weather that week, and the pot of chocolate Heidi had made. It was some time before Dr. Churchill could sort out what each of us recalled about the *egg*, its whereabouts, and any special interest shown in it by strange bears visiting the shop.

Finally I asked him to tell us what he thought, and he addressed himself to all of us.

"Friends," he said, "the egg is gone. It may have been gone for a considerable period of time. Now, where did it go? Unless I am mistaken, it didn't leave here by itself—it would have to be a remarkable egg indeed to do that, eh, Goods? And I believe it didn't leave in the pocket of a shoplifter—not only did no bear here see signs of any shoplifter but there are, everywhere in the shop, many more valuable, smaller items that are easier to carry off and sell. From remarks Ophelia and Zenobia have made now and then, I gather other things are missing as well. I am drawn to a conclusion: The egg was stolen by someone we all know."

Here Clarence said, "Oh, no, surely not," and Zenobia nudged him and whispered, "Think of the berry jars, Clarence," but she grew pale as Dr. Churchill proceeded. He turned to Mona Lisa and said, "The likeliest suspects are those who have three things in common: a trained collector's eye, access, and a motive. Mona Lisa, my dear, step here, please. You are such a bear. You bring beautifully chosen odds and ends into the shop and always admire the best things here, and you must be in need of money." I wanted to protest and defend Mona Lisa, who looked stricken, but before I could speak Dr. Churchill said, "Conrad, who appeared in this month's window, and who isn't here today, is another such bear." I heard Zenobia gasp. "He is a collector. He has rich tastes, and his glove was found near where the egg was last seen." He gestured toward the table. Clarence said, "Dr.

Churchill . . ." but Dr. Churchill said, "Wait just a minute and I'll be through. The investment bear—what is his name? Yes, Jean de Noël—was here on the day the egg was seen for the last time. He sailed immediately for a foreign port. He strikes me as a suspicious character. For instance, I have seen his eyes rove through the shop, taking everything in, while he seemed to be engaged in intimate conversation. Finally, and it breaks my heart to name someone of whom I've grown so fond and think so well—there is Ricky Jaune. Ricky is a young bear who has

RICKY JAUNE AND M. RITZ

OPHELIA'S DESK FOR MAY

lately taken up pinball, an expensive and addictive game. He has made doubtful friends. He is often alone in the shop. Ricky, step—" But Ricky had burst into tears and was flying out the door, stammering, "I didn't do it. I thought you were my friend," as he ran. At that moment Dr. Churchill seemed to see, for the first time, that everyone was shaken or in tears. He ran his paw across his chin, said, "Maybe I . . ." and turned and took off after Ricky.

Ricky was found by him that night, sitting in the Champ-de-Mars, across from the Ecole Militaire, with a tear-stained face and M. Ritz on his knee murmuring gentle consolations. Dr. Churchill talked to Ricky for a long time and then took him by the paw to La Coupole for late supper. They sat and worked things out between them, and they were friends again. The next day Dr. Churchill had to leave with Mr. Goods for England, but before he took his train he came to our house and apologized for letting his professional manner outweigh his sensitivity to our feelings. He knew we were all friends; it was what he had loved so much about being with us these two months. He was contrite. His deductions weren't wrong, he said, but they were tactless; and now he was convinced that Ricky Jaune, at least, was innocent. He asked me to keep him informed of all developments, especially about Ricky, and said that he would think about the case and write to us.

That day Zenobia made us promise not to tell Conrad or Jean de Noël or anyone else what had taken place. Too many people had had their feelings hurt, she said. For the time being we should try to put the egg from our minds and just be a little more alert and cautious. We all agreed, but I could not help but wonder what Conrad had been worrying over that evening at the Dilettante. Why did he always wear those gloves and why was Mona upset about them? For she trembled now whenever she saw he had them on. What explained Mona's own odd behavior in the shop? And, most important, were Jean de Noël's eyes really "roving" while he talked to me and paid me compliments?

As I write I hear Zenobia calling me to help Marcello climb up into the window, and I go, happy it's May.

MAY 2   On the spur of the moment, because of the warm weather, Marcello and I decide to give a musical evening at the Italian embassy—on the 7th! I send out all the invitations right away.

A Musical Evening
with
The charismatic Ambassador to Rome
Signor Marcello
Entertainments and La Dolce Vita
9 o'clock   May 7
R.S.V.P.

my dear signorina,

Count me in,

Vincent

CARTOLINA POSTALE ITALIANA
(CARTE POSTALE D'ITALIE.)

Edit. A. Mozzi, Firenze

Ophelia B.
Elise
7 bis rue des
Bears
Seattle Paris

operas on his piano, and when
Heidi and Clafouti brought out an
ice-cream cake modeled on the
Coliseum, he raised a spun-sugar
scepter and declared the evening
"la dolce vita." Popi, as
M. V. de Paul calls himself when
he's dressed up, didn't eat a piece
of the cake—like a hermit,
he eats only bread—but he read
tarot cards in a corner in his robes
and predicted great things for
Camille and for myself.

MAY 5   M. V. de Paul, a Roman
acquaintance of Marcello's, showed up this
morning in the most amazing liturgical robes.
Like John and Benedict, he thinks he is a true
pope, exiled, and like Saint Francis he believes
he has the stigmata—in this case, a pink patch
on his stomach. After blessing each of us, he
threw the attaché's espresso pots out the
window and climbed in himself, so now we
have an imperial "pope-entate" reigning from
the center of the window and a poor, courtly
diplomat crowded off into a corner.

MAY 8   Our musical evening at the
embassy was thronged with Italian bears and
all our friends. The pasta disappeared before
the music started; the calzone and zeppole were
gobbled by the score. Camille was there,
looking beautiful but downcast, for she still
hasn't been offered any parts to dance in the
ballet. Albert and Anemone were there too.
Marcello played melodies from early Italian

DAMA DI DENARI

DAMA DI DENARI

POPIE AS A BABY

MARCELLO, AMBASSADOR TO ROME

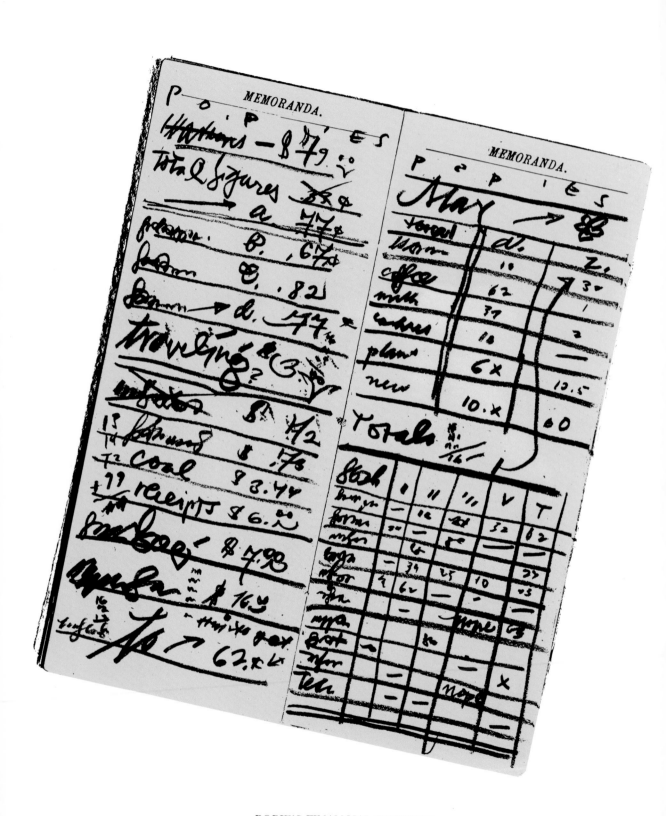

POPIE'S FINANCIAL RECORDS

MAY 13   A taxi pulled up to the shop this morning, and the driver, with his eyes wide on Popi in the window, handed me a basket of *muguets.* Among the flowers was a small, lamé-wrapped box, and inside the box was an antique garnet pendant surrounded by a set of perfect Bohemian stones and lying on top of it was a note addressed to me. The note said, "This is a small token of my admiration. Will you have dinner with me on the 28th, when I return to Paris? Your much honored, Jean de Noël." My heart fluttered. Then Clarence walked in and I thought: I cannot keep the stones, I know, but can a bear so generous be anything but honest and true-hearted?

MAY 22   Moshe and Golda will arrive from America next week! This is a surprise. They are old family friends from the days when my father, my mother, and I lived in Tibet. Golda and Moshe are Russian exiles who lost their fortune and became *marchands,* as I am now, until they found an "old master" among a lot of books and paintings they had the good fortune to buy sight unseen, many years ago. They now keep a suite of rooms in the Hotel Pierre in New York and are coming to Paris to bring me back to New York with them to celebrate their fiftieth anniversary there. The only thing that won't be flown in for the party

from our old haunts, they write, will be the emblematical ice carvings. New York! Who could resist the temptation to go?

MAY 28   I read in the paper today that a bank in Rome, the Banca Gelateria, has closed its doors. The bank did not keep books. The central figure in the scandal is named M. V. de Paolo, and his picture looks very much like our own Popi. Is it possible that Popi is in disguise? I know he is not a financial wizard. Zenobia helped him to balance his checkbook last week and made a bet with him for ten pounds of chocolates he couldn't keep it balanced by himself. She was chuckling about it afterward. She said she had never seen numbers so bent and strained in all her life. She was almost sure of winning.

MAY 29   I had dinner with Jean de Noël last night. It was a balmy, starlit evening. The dinner was over quickly, and Jean de Noël was off on business once again; but he was so attentive and gallant while it lasted that he sort of bewitched me, and I let him kiss me when we reached my door. That's when I thought of Clarence. But does Clarence care? I am beginning to like Jean de Noël—perhaps too much.

june

MOSHE AND GOLDA

J U N E

JUNE 1   Preparations for the arrival of Moshe and Golda are in full swing this morning, and nothing else is on our minds! M. Ritz has gone to rent a limousine; Clarence is making a menu for a special dinner on Wednesday, to be ordered from Potel et Chabot; and Ricky, with great energy, is sweeping diplomatic dispatches and holy water from the window, where, tomorrow, I hope Moshe and Golda will pose in public celebration of their fifty years of mutual affection. This will by my surprise for *them*.

JUNE 2   Moshe and Golda are thrilled with the city, the street, the shop, and the window. They came directly from the airport in a taxi, laden with a dozen trunks and suitcases for their five-day stay. They have not changed! Moshe, putting down some small bags in the doorway, threw open his arms and said, "Ophie! How we've missed you! And your shop! It's a *goisa oytser!*" (Later he explained to me this means a treasure chest from heaven.) Golda whisked past him and kissed me. Then she took my arm and bustled me from table to table, asking me questions about everything she saw. When she came upon a group of little brass figures, she said, "Ophie, you still have some of your mother's things," and, holding a gilded bronze Buddha in her paw, regaled the customers and the postman, who was delivering our letters, with stories of the dangers and delights of Lhasa. This pleased the postman, who had once handled a cable addressed to someone in that city but could

never believe that such an exotic-sounding place existed.

Moshe and Golda went to unpack their bags at their hotel; then they returned and we fed them. Now they are standing cuddled up together in the window, re-creating their wedding pictures. Long-stemmed roses lie all around them. M. Ritz and Ricky brought the roses, explaining as they snipped the stems that the gardeners in the rose garden of Bagatelle just happened to be pruning as the two of them walked by. I thought, Those gardeners certainly are pruning early! Oh, well, if M. Grandiose, who I see is slipping a rosebud in his coat lapel, asked them no questions, neither shall I.

JUNE 4   Last night, as we sat down to Clarence's beautifully chosen dinner of soufflés, meringues, and custards, we each found an envelope containing airline tickets peeking out from underneath our butter plates. *Everyone* is invited to Moshe and Golda's anniversary party in New York! Today, no one in the house can talk of anything but getting ready for the trip. Even Heidi and Clafouti, who cannot come, poor dears, because one of their friends has a show of paintings in two weeks, are excited and spent the morning helping me look for my high-topped walking shoes beneath the beds and armchairs. When, sneezing and covered with dust, they found them and handed them to me, they didn't even complain about the dust. It was my turn to clean last week, but as I sometimes do, I forgot. Ricky volunteered to iron the ruffles on my dresses, and then

Clarence, who is looking forward to trying American food (I can hear him humming, "Mares eat grits, and does eat grits, and little lambs eat home fries," from the kitchen as I write), took Ricky out to buy his very first suit. Ricky looks completely different in it—devilish, respectable, *distingué*, and sweet.

JUNE 10   Zenobia won her bet. We are eating chocolates by the pawful.

JUNE 12   Moshe and Golda, Heidi and Clafouti, Albert, Anemone, Ricky, and Camille are out seeing Paris in the "compact" limousine M. Ritz brought home, and so I am alone when Clarence lets himself into the salon this evening, humming a melancholy tune. I say hello to him and he says, "Oh, it's you,

Ophelia. I didn't see you." When I ask if something is wrong, he says, "No, nothing's wrong. I can't come to New York, that's all," as he throws his jacket down and heads toward the kitchen.

I follow him and find him slumped in a chair, absently letting a fly buzz around his head and light on his left ear. "Can you really not come to New York, Clarence?" I ask. "Did something happen?"

"Too much to do," he says. "Opening of a new restaurant on boulevard Montparnasse. Guest chef at the Brasserie Lipp. Visit to Paris by my publisher's niece, who wants *apprendre à escribouiller*, as she puts it—to learn to review food as I do. I just met her at dinner, Ophelia. She weighs three hundred pounds. The publisher won't let me off."

"Oh, Clarence," I say, "what a disappointment!" We console each other for a while, and then, wanting him not to become *too* melancholy, I put my arms around him and tickle him to make him laugh.

JUNE 17   New York! We are in the elegant, small Elysée Hotel on East Fifty-fourth Street, with the Waldorf-Astoria and Lutèce down a few streets and F.A.O. Schwarz, Rumpelmayer's, and Central Park uptown on Fifth Avenue. Ricky, Zenobia, and I—only we!—point and chatter as we walk along. There is the Plaza Hotel, and there, across Fifty-eighth Street, is the site where those famous American industrialist bears, the Vanderbilts and Whitneys, outdid the age of progress itself by building a conclave of 137-room houses. As we stroll and lick our street-

OPHELIA'S DESK FOR JUNE

vendor's ice-cream cones, we spot the Hotel Pierre, where the cleaning bears and waiters are, we imagine, getting ready for the party this evening. I must get organized, I tell myself, taking out a little note pad to make a list as we walk on toward the zoo. There is much to do: (1) Help Zenobia to find fawn-colored shoes to match her dress. (2) Buy ribbons from Cherchez and order more. (3) Wrap Moshe and Golda's anniversary present (a crystal perfume flacon, etched in gold in the Russian way, that I have saved for a long time). (4) Comb my fur *after* I put on my dress, and wind as many ribbons through it as I can.

JUNE 19   The anniversary party was wonderful. We think it was the best party ever. It chimed and rustled on until almost morning, when everyone still there was given bluebells (the flower of unending love) to toss in the path of Moshe and Golda as they ascended to their suite of rooms. The lobby was an avenue lined with corkscrew willows strung with threads of lights and golden ribbons leading to the ballroom and the dining room. Dinner was served at midnight, on deep blue plates rimmed with gold, and conversation among the five hundred guests (five hundred!) was animated. Golda cut the anniversary cake of brown sugar, butter, currants, and nuts, frosted with candied mimosas, and afterward she and Moshe led the Russian country dances. We danced until the light of dawn began to streak the windows.

As Zenobia, I, Ricky, and an old collecting friend of ours were leaving the hotel, I caught sight of the catering manager, Pierre Granuler,

who worked for many years at the George V in Paris. I greeted him and told him how sorry Clarence would be not to see him; told him about Clarence's publisher's niece; told him he was one of the very few chefs Clarence had ever taken into his confidence. He smiled and shook his head and said, "I don't think I'm the only one who knows Clarence is "Les Comestibles," if that is what you mean, my dear. Clarence's secret is not much of a secret, at least in the hotels of Paris. But we like to humor him, you know!" Oh, dear, I shan't tell that to Clarence!

JUNE 21   Ricky loves New York. He has been to SoHo, to late-night punk rock clubs in Chelsea, and even to the Brooklyn Esplanade across the river. But Zenobia and I saw Mayor Koch! He was eating rum-raisin ice cream, while we were eating almond crunch, in Peppermint Park, and he shook our paws and winked.

JUNE 22   The desk clerk at the Elysée hands me two letters as I pass through the black-and-white-tiled lobby on my way to meet Zenobia, Moshe, and Golda at the Russian Tea Room on West Fifty-seventh Street for lunch. One is from Marcello, and although his handwriting is very hard to read, I extract from it surprising news: Jean de Noël has followed me to New York! He visited the embassy the day after we left, having learned from the countess that Clarence had to stay at home; and he closeted himself with M. V. de Paul to talk about the cocoa-bean market. Jean told Popi he might as well do some business while he was pursuing ("the woman of his dreams" or "wonderful schemes"?) in New York.

I don't read my other letter or even become nervous about Jean de Noël, because Ricky is waiting for me at the mahagony-and-beveled-glass revolving door that is the entrance to the Russian Tea Room. He is perspiring. He has walked all the way from Wall Street, where he has just *seen* Jean de Noël in the lunchtime crowd, flanked by two tall gray-suited stock-broker bears. Did I know that he was here?

Now I am nervous—and excited.

After lunch I open the other envelope in which nestles a little postcard from Clarence. "Having a wonderful time," he writes in wavering letters. Oh, stoic, darling bear!

I go and pick out brass blazer buttons, monogrammed with little *C*'s, at a charming shop called Tender Buttons, to make it up to him.

JUNE 27   I have seen Jean de Noël—six times, to tell the complete truth. He calls every evening at our hotel. Zenobia says he is paying court to me—but she says it with a little frown, as though it's troublesome. Is she remembering what Dr. Churchill said? Or does she think he's too short for me? He is charming. On the evening of the day Ricky caught a glimpse of him on Wall Street, he pulled up at the Elysée in a horse-drawn hansom cab. We rode into the park and had a champagne picnic. The next evening he took me to a peaches-and-ice-cream party high in a house overlooking the Hudson River and the sunset and introduced me to the hostess as "the beautiful Ophelia." On the night after that, supper at Bonte bakery on Third Avenue; the next night, the ballet.

When I speak—oh, of the color of the sky, or the sweetness of American strawberries, or a snow-white piece of statuary Zenobia and I came across in a little shop on Second Avenue—Jean de Noël listens with deference, with light in his black eyes and a slight bowing of his head. He tells me stories of great financial transactions—the secreting of recipes in mergers of large chocolate houses, the fall of banks and mammoth honey farms—and if the stories, and he, sometimes sound a little, well, worldly, then that must be because he is a bear of the world and thinks as such bears do. He is gallant. If a waiter seems to slight me or someone on the streets stares openly at me as we pass by, he will demand a full apology, which the waiter or the bear on the street always gives. It's true this is a little embarrassing, but he means well. And his eyes *don't* rove.

JUNE 28   Zenobia and I had breakfast in the Café des Artistes this morning, handsome with its Howard Chandler Christy murals, wood paneling, and air of an old men's club. As we were deciding what we would crowd into our last two days, we laughingly agreed: We won't go home! We'll stay in New York for another week! The Bazaar des Bears will be all right; Ricky will be happy; Zenobia will have time to visit farther-flung museums and to find out about the bookkeeping methods of the Bronx Zoo, which she's been curious about. And I will eat ice cream on the streets, walk miles in high-topped shoes, and dance under the New York stars all night—just once.

We go to see Moshe and Golda, and they make our new reservations. July 8!

july

OPHELIA'S DESK

J U L Y

JULY 4   Pinwheels and starbursts break through the dark sky above Central Park and a hundred smaller parks and copper and parapeted rooftops downtown. "Almost like *Le Quatorze Juillet* in Paris!" Zenobia calls, with high approbation for her—from across the roof of the Palace Hotel, where Jean de Noël has brought us for the wide, round view. Moshe and Golda clap their paws; Ricky cheers; and I blush with confusion as, under cover of the noise and lights, Jean de Noël whispers compliments in my ear.

JULY 6   A letter from Heidi and Clafouti: They have kept the shop and the house well dusted, they write, and have started to assemble flags and ribbons for the Bazaar's Bastille Day window. They have not picked out the portraits of eighteenth-century heroic *révolutionnaire* bears, however, because they

want to save that for me to do when I come home. (Does this mean that Marie Antoinette and the Empress Josephine may not have to be given the center spot this year?) When *are* we coming home? they ask. They and M. Ritz and Clarence and the count and countess miss us.

JULY 7   Jean de Noël cannot fly home with us. "I want to buy a few more cocoa contracts," he explains. He holds my paw at our farewell dinner at Pâtisserie Lanciana and says he will hurry to Paris as soon as his business is done.

JULY 10   We are home! In fact, I am writing from the shop. It is dim and clean and quiet, and it feels to me like a nest of sweet, familiar treasures.

  Our trip was an adventure. On our last morning in New York, Moshe and Golda surprised us with tickets on the Concorde for our flight. We zoomed out to the airport and snuggled into the big, comfortable seats of the plane, and we didn't realize that we were homesick until we'd settled down. Then we asked the stewardess for everything we wanted: melons, playing cards, fruit punch, cold fish, French newspapers, walnuts, a chess set, and sleep shades (for Zenobia). Ricky, dressed in his new suit, asked for *Barron's*, the *Wall Street Journal*, *The Economist*, doing a good imitation of an American businessman; I think he was flirting with the stewardess. Soon, he became engrossed in reading, and after a while, just as Zenobia and I were beginning a game of

"Fish," he gasped and said, "Ophelia, listen to this report from the *New York Times*! 'Four hundred to six hundred American black wild Western bears, who usually eat ants and ground beetles and dig up wasps' nests' "— ugh!—" 'have been pilfering food from national parks campers—usually by guile and often by intimidation.' How do you like that? 'The bears are known as "panhandlers." A number of them wait along hikers' trails. Once a hiker sits down and doffs his backpack, a bear dashes from the underbrush, seizes the pack, and makes off into the woods with the hiker's food.' "

"What kind of food?" Zenobia said.

"It doesn't say, but it must be tastier than ground *beetles*. 'Sometimes they resort to intimidation,' " Ricky read on. " 'This translates into what park rangers call the "bluff charge," in which the bears confront a hiker with loud snorts, charge, slide to a stop, snap their jaws and say "Woof." For most city dwellers, this is enough to make their knees turn to jelly. It causes them to shed their packs in order to run faster. This is just what the bears want.' "

"I should think so!" Zenobia said.

"Clarence once saw a movie in which two American bears had to rob a farmhouse just to get a little flour to make bread. He thought it was a historical movie. *Pour l'amour de Dieu!* I didn't know the American West was still like that," I said.

"They don't seem to have houses, either," Ricky said. "They can't cook! Listen to this: 'The more the bears get accustomed to real food, the more trouble there is.' But what *should* they be accustomed to?" There was a white-suited stranger with his arm in a sling and a patch over one eye sidling up the aisle as Ricky spoke. He was pretending to look out the windows at the clouds, but I could see that he was listening to us. Step by step, he approached the back of Ricky's seat as Ricky read: " 'The parks are full of signs warning against feeding the bears. There are fines of up to fifty dollars. . . .' "

"Ho-hummm!" The strange bear, directly behind Ricky now, cleared his throat, and both Ricky and Zenobia, who had not seen him coming, jumped. "I thought I recognized you folks. Pardon me if I surprised you. My name is Brady B. Boeing, and I called upon you once before. My card." He handed me a calling card. He said, "Your store was recommended to me by Mr. Jean Noël. Pleased to meet you," and he stuck out his good paw to each of us in turn. We couldn't help but notice his oversized gold watch.

"Now," he said, "I overheard you talking, especially since you were talking about *my* part of the country, the western United States, and I'd like to straighten you out about a couple of things. What you're talking about when you talk about those bears, though you may not know it, are hobos."

JEAN DE NOEL

CLARENCE AND DR. CHURCHILL

"What do you mean?" Ricky said, and I saw Zenobia's ears perk up. This was Americana.

"Why, those bears like to pretend to be hungry, young man. But there are *thousands* of ants and wasps out there, all public property. Those bears are free to eat them." Ricky started to say, "Well, would you trade places?" but Brady Boeing said, "No! They'll never be happy. They are romantics and that's the end of it"; and he threw himself into the seat next to mine, looking highly satisfied with himself beneath his eyepatch. Then he told us stories about the West.

When the Concorde landed—even though Zenobia poked her elbow in my ribs—I invited Brady Boeing to visit us in the shop. But when he said, "Why ten herds of wild buffaloes and a barrel of scorpions couldn't keep me away," even I had pause. Ugh!

JULY 14   Bastille Day, and Clarence reserved a table for us on a *bateau mouche*, so we watch the fireworks—the second in a month!—as we drift in the twilight Seine. And who do you think is with us, sitting a little apart with Zenobia, shyly taking her paw in his? It is Conrad. I gave him a lecture yesterday—well, sort of. I saw him on the boulevard St.-Germain for the first time since Dr. Churchill sailed; and when he ducked his head and pretended not to see me, I snuck up, put my arms around him and told him that we missed him. He must have heard about the doctor's inquest and the egg, and perhaps he thought we didn't want to see him. He called for Zenobia this morning, and he was not wearing gloves.

This is the first Quatorze Juillet of M. Dilettante, and after the fireworks we walk to his shop to help him celebrate in a true French way. Soon, though the shop is small, we are dancing—I with Clarence, Camille (beautifully) with the proprietor, Albert with Anemone, and Zenobia (bashfully) with Conrad. We whirl and pirouette, and then, suddenly, Jean de Noël is standing in the doorway—in just the same calm, dark way he stood on the day we caught the butterflies. He touches his friend M. Dilettante's shoulder as he makes his way to Clarence and me. He takes me gracefully from Clarence's arms. Clarence looks angry as we spin past him, but Jean de Noël whispers in my ear, "Pay no attention. Think only of me."

Conrad walks Zenobia home, and I hear her humming allemandes as she goes to bed.

JULY 21   The postman delivers a note from Dr. Churchill just as I discover that my Paris *métro* pass is lost. Dr. Churchill and his aunt Vita will visit on September 5. I write back to say how glad I am and that Ricky often speaks of him, has given up pinball, and is happy as a clam.

JULY 30   Well, we are taking another vacation! Clarence made reservations for us at a seaside inn in Provence for the summer holidays in two weeks, and he says that anyone

OPHELIA

who wants to can come along—except Jean de Noël! Those are his terms, Clarence says. "I'm not going to have that little Napoleon rushing around me, giving out gifts to every female bear he sees." I didn't argue with him, because Jean must stay in Paris for the month on business, anyway. But Clarence is certainly peevish. I saw him throw away two perfectly good boxes of Le Dilettante chocolates two days ago, and last night he ferociously forbade Ricky Jaune to buy any more. Still, he promises we'll gather ingredients for potpourri in Provence and visit all the flea markets, and this morning he did find my pass.

August

ZENOBIA WITH BRADY BOEING AND M. RITZ

A U G U S T

AUGUST 3   "Well . . . what about these little wooden packing cases?" Clarence is saying, holding one of the jar-sized wooden crates up to the light slanting through the curtained window of the shop. "Didn't you say you threw them away, Zenobia?" There is a grumpy note of bafflement creeping into Clarence's voice.

"Yes," Zenobia says, "I *did*. That's the oddest part. It was raining on the afternoon the

M. RITZ

berry jars were delivered—that was in November—and everything was wet. The postman was wet, the cases were wet, and even the jars were wet. There was a customer in the shop, and I gave Monsieur Ritz the paper wrappings and the cases to throw away while I waited on her. She bought a bead—one glass bead." Zenobia's memory is always prodigious.

"Did you throw them away out back, Monsieur Ritz?" I ask, hoping our mouse's memory will be jogged. He is seated on the top trestle of Zenobia's desk chair, his little legs crossed and his little paws joggling. I am seated at my desk. "Can you remember?" I say.

M. Ritz takes a pencil from his ear, his note pad from the chair post beside him, and writes upon his knee: "I put the *papers* in the back. I put the boxes in front, under the tree, for the dormice to find in case they needed winter houses."

"That was thoughtful, Monsieur Ritz," Zenobia, who has come and leaned over his shoulder, says. "He says he put them out front, Clarence," she calls toward the window, where Clarence is standing. "Under the tree," I add, then ask, "The sidewalk or the *égout* side, Monsieur Ritz?"

"Does it make a difference?" Clarence asks as M. Ritz scribbles *sidewalk*. "Front or back, whatever . . . the important thing is that last November the boxes the berry jars were shipped in were put outside the shop, the jars themselves were inside, and then they disappeared; now boxes and jars are returned and reunited, like eggshells and eggs, like Cinderella and her shoe. Ophelia, are you *sure* these are the same jars?" he asks.

"I'm sure," I say for the second time. I think Clarence is still in a bad mood. I turn one of the green-and-blue enameled jars over on my desk and point to the pencil marks on the bottom in Zenobia's round handwriting: *From Liege. November 27. Number 3.* Clarence strolls over, looks, shrugs, and then begins to pace. "And Ricky didn't see anyone carrying a package in this morning?" he says.

Zenobia tells him no and reminds him that the only time *any* of us were out of the shop was when we were rescuing "that

unpredictable American bear," Brady Boeing.

That's right, I think, we all *were* gone from the shop together for a little while this morning.

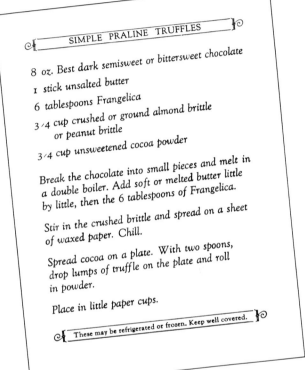

We were about to taste the chocolate truffles Zenobia had made from a recipe charmed out of M. Dilettante for Conrad's birthday, which is tomorrow, when suddenly we heard a clamor in the street. We ran outside and saw a crowd of children rounding the corner, shouting, "*Un pirate!*" and pulling at the coattails of a bantam bear with a patch on his eye and his arm in a sling, who was hollering "Let go of me!" in a Texas twang while the

OPHELIA'S DESK FOR AUGUST

FERMETURE ANNUELLE

children reached for his eyepatch. I thought I heard Zenobia chuckle once as I sprinted to the shop for a plate of her chocolates to coax the children with (How unlike Zenobia! I thought), and by the time Ricky and I had bribed the children and secured Brady Boeing and helped him, bedraggled, into the shop, we had all been gone ten minutes. Someone could have crept in then! It was only a little while later, after we'd cut a new eyepatch from black blotting paper, that Zenobia found the berry jars. They were lined up in their boxes on the shelf beneath the counter where we keep our ribbons, tea, chocolate, and sugar. Zenobia was about to begin to make her truffles over again. The children had eaten all of them—a sound endorsement.

"Zenobia," I say now, "do you think someone brought the jars and boxes back while we were helping Brady Boeing?"

"That could be," Zenobia says. "But who?"

"Well, we know it wasn't Ricky," I say. "We can report *that* to Dr. Churchill."

Clarence stops his pacing and smiles for the first time in six days. "I've got an idea," he says. "Let's all go out and wander around, and maybe by the time we come back we'll find— what else beside the crystal egg is missing, Zenobia?"

The mention of the crystal egg seems to have a dispiriting effect upon Zenobia. Is she thinking about Conrad? Does she suspect him? She says, "Oh, let's not talk about it now," and, picking up her round straw hat and

80

handing mine to me, declares, "Let's go and get ice-cream parfaits for lunch."

M. Ritz gestures that he will stay and keep watch until we return, and we pad out the door.

But who brought back the berry jars? I think. And why, after all these months?

We eat three ice-cream parfaits apiece and buy one more—praline, M. Ritz's favorite flavor.

ZENOBIA

AUGUST 5   At seven-thirty last evening, Albert and Anemone, their horse, M. Dilettante, Camille, Heidi, Clafouti, Ricky, Brady Boeing, Clarence, Jean de Noël, and I hid behind our peach and yellow chairs until the doorbell rang. Then we jumped out at Conrad. He ducked his head and smiled as we applauded. Zenobia handed him the white, beribboned box of homemade truffles, and he shyly held out a big brown box to her, saying, "I wanted you to have a present too, Zenobia." As Zenobia tipped the lid and peeked inside, we could hear faint humming. "A lawn mower," Brady Boeing said. "His heart," said Jean de Noël with a wink, and Camille giggled and said, "Oh, Monsieur de Noël!" Meanwhile a look of rapt surprise was filling Zenobia's face. The humming grew a little louder, and just as Clarence and I were both about to ask, "What is it?" a fragment of humming detached itself, escaped the box, became a buzzing and then became a bee. A bee! A hive of bees! Conrad, shyness gone with a call upon him for action, tripped over and plucked it out of the air by the back of its two wings, dropped it into the box, and smiled. Zenobia, smiling too and flushing, placed a kiss on Conrad's furry cheek, and we cheered as they stood and beamed at each other. M.

South, top flower, red

OPHELIA

BRADY B. BOEING

Dilettante tasted one of Conrad's birthday chocolates, blew a kiss into the air, shook Zenobia's paw, offered her a job, peered into the box of bees, pretended to faint, and then we cut the cake.

This morning, after I had shown out of the shop some Rheims bears, who bought a pretty piece of lace, Zenobia, sitting at her desk, feeding sunflowers to her bees, said, "You know, Ophelia, I think I'd better stay in Paris for the holidays. Someone ought to watch the shop." I pretended to be surprised and saddened and didn't tell her that I knew Conrad would be staying, too, or that I knew she couldn't bear *(ahem)* to leave her bees.

AUGUST 10   We are in a little farmhouse outside of Aix-en-Provence. Beneath our windows, fields of cabbages and carnations slope down to the orchards and the woods beyond. It is so restful! We are staying with a light-furred, round-faced family who like to be our guides. This morning they showed us patches of wild lavender, rosemary, and thyme. We picked enough to fill our hats and pockets, and Ricky slipped some underneath our pillows, to scent our sleep and dreams.

AUGUST 11   The potpourri didn't work on Clarence! He is *still* a grouch. This morning, walking into town, he didn't say a word to me—until I stopped along the road to pick a *bleuet* that was growing in a flowerbed near a stone fence. Then he said, "Hurry *up.*" Now, how could he know that I was thinking of Jean de Noël?

Later in M. Du Sucre's candy shop, Clarence was gruff and snappish. He was making a study of local candied violets and he said to me, "Here. Taste one of these and tell me what you think." I took one of the delicate little flowers from his paw, bit into it, and said, "Mmm—*délicieux,*" reaching for another. Clarence snatched it back. "Bah!" he said. "They're awful! What's happened to you, Ophelia? You used to have good taste," and stomping out of the store, he muttered, "*Bleuets, bleuets, bleuets.*"

I followed him and called, "Nothing's happened to my taste, Clarence! But something's happened to your manners! Monsieur Du Sucre could have heard you, you know! You're turning into a rude bear! And you're jealous!" I wasn't sure that this was true, but it made me feel better to say it.

By that time Clarence's blond back was disappearing down the street. I took my time. This was the closest to a real fight Clarence and I have ever had.

AUGUST 12   "I think I may owe you an apology," Clarence says, holding what I am sure is another winning cribbage hand close to his blond chest.

"Oh, really, Clarence?" I say, laying down a card.

"Don't be sassy, Ophelia. I think we should have a talk when we get back to Paris." He places a three of hearts atop his pile of cards.

"All right," I say, looking at my hand with new sanguinity and putting down the first five I've had in the game. "Fifteen-two." Ha, ha.

AUGUST 18   When Heidi and Clafouti and I grow restless this morning, we take a picnic lunch of peaches deep into the woods to look for hazelnuts. Here Heidi finds, in a chain of dark caves below a green glade, an ancient shrine to Saint Bearnadelle! Beneath the portrait, carved with a wide blade, is the motto: *D'avantage est rarement suffisant.* We are pleased, and notify the bishop.

AUGUST 28   We are at home again—and sleepy! With all the sun we took and all the fruit and honey we ate, we can barely rouse ourselves from our little beds this morning. We linger over our brioches. By the time I get to the shop, it is like a busy dovecote or cocoon of moths: Zenobia and Brady Boeing are chattering about aerodynamics together in the window, while Zenobia's bees, out of the hive "for exercise," are flying back and forth behind her, appearing to kiss her on the neck from time to time. Inside the shop, Camille, brighter and more animated than I've seen her since she left the Ballet Ours, is dancing arabesques for the postman, who taps his paw and twirls his hat in time to "The Dance of the Sugar Plum Fairies," which Camile is humming as she dances. They run to kiss me hello, and then Camille tells me of her unexpected good luck: A rich bear, she says, "a generous and, oh, so handsome bear, Ophelia," has underwritten a fall production of *The Nutcracker Suite*, "but only if I dance the lead! He says I'm born to be a star and Paris is crazy not to know it yet!"

CAMILLE

"That's wonderful, Camille," I say. "Who is he?"

"Oh, I can't tell you *that*," she says. "He made me promise not to tell. But the production is in November, and I promise you I'll get you front-row seats. You too, Monsieur Gris. Oh, I'm so excited!"

The postman looks a little uncomfortable as he fumbles in his satchel for my letters. I wonder why. Does he know who Camille's mysterious benefactor is? Hmmm. Just one more mystery.

september

AUNT VITA WITH OPHELIA

S E P T E M B E R

SEPTEMBER 1   Today M. Ritz outwitted two big stray cats who walked into the shop looking confident and mean. As soon as they made a move toward the sugar supplies, M. Ritz stood, paws on hips, and squeeked at them; they yowled and took off after him like furry comets. All of them vanished in a whirlwind down the *métro* stairway across the street, and by the time I got there the ticket-taking bear was laughing very hard. M. Ritz had raced the cats onto the platform and kept them running around in circles until the train pulled in. Then, quick as a wink, he darted in one door and out another, just as it was sliding closed. The last the ticket taker saw of the cats, they were peering disconsolately from a train window, heading toward porte Maillot.

SEPTEMBER 6   Dr. Churchill and his aunt Vita arrived yesterday, and Ricky Jaune checked them into a pretty little hotel around the corner from us on the rue Vaneau. Ricky and Dr. Churchill are really fond of each other; I could see it by the way they both tugged shyly but resolutely at Aunt Vita's heaviest carpetbag, murmuring, "Oh, no. Let me take that." Dr. Churchill kept saying jovially, "Well, Well! Ricky Jaune! And how is our young friend?" And Ricky kept running ahead of the porter to show the Churchills the sights of the hotel, which he had chosen.

Clarence met us at three for peppermint tea. He had just finished writing an essay on the southern fruit flies that are turning up in this season's fruit purées (he found two the day before in his cherry soufflé), and at first he was in a happy mood; but when Dr. Churchill, Aunt Vita, and Ricky rose to go, he said in a low voice, "Ophelia, stay. I want to have a word with you."

I said, "*Mais, certainement*, Clarence," and arranged to meet Aunt Vita at the shop at five o'clock to see which of our sets of tea things she would like to pose with in the window. I thought: This is going to be Clarence's and my talk together! I love talks. When everyone was gone, he said:

AUNT VITA

DR. CHURCHILL

"May I ask you a question, Ophelia?"

"Yes," I said, but my heart jumped. Clarence almost never asked me formal questions. He told me things he thinks I ought to know.

"Good. First, then: Do you consider yourself to be in love with Jean de Noël?"

Uh-oh, I thought then. I said, "I don't know." I didn't know. I hadn't seen Jean de Noël very often since we came back to Paris—only once or twice on the stairs of the *hôtel particulier*. I told myself he must be very busy with his fall investments, but I wasn't sure of this. I often thought of his saying, "Beautiful Ophelia!" I didn't want to talk about it.

"Perhaps a little bit," I said.

"Oh, Ophelia," Clarence replied, so sorrowfully that my pulse beat faster still. Did Clarence really care if I did love Jean de Noël? Could it be *true* that he was jealous?

No. Chin in paw, Clarence meditated for a moment and then said: "It's difficult for me to tell you this, especially since I don't have concrete evidence. But I'm pretty sure that Jean de Noël is a *coquin*, a Casanova, Ophelia. A chef I know in the Champs-Elysées tells me that he dines there with a different female bear every week or two. Have you ever noticed anything peculiar about his behavior when you're with him?"

"No," I said, my feelings already beginning to be hurt, "except that he tells me I'm *pretty* and likes to have me all to himself."

"Ah, jealous—thinks everyone's as he is. Do you take that as a compliment? It's not. Well, never mind. What *I've* noticed is that in the shop, at Le Dilettante on Bastille Day, even in our rooms at home, he looks at other bears, smiles at them, and poses for them—even while he's dancing with theatrical grace with *you*. I once saw him glinting at Zenobia! Dr. Churchill noticed it. Remember? Now, I don't necessarily think that Jean de Noël is a thief, mind you, but I do think that he's a playboy. What made me sure was overhearing Heidi and Clafouti fretting about it—about his amorous glances at another bear during Conrad's birthday party, before we went away.

When I interrupted and asked them who it was, they were startled and wouldn't tell me—were afraid I'd tell you, I guess. For a long

September 6th

Vita arrives with enough
clutter for a year's visit
rather than a month... such
a dear, constantly mutter...
about being too much trou...
which she couldn't possibl...
be aside from the fact
that her complete occupa-
tion with her camera tak...
her off on some field tri...
or other most every day, e...
confided that she may ne...
glasses as her pictures h...
a bit out of focus, howeve...
I didn't mention that her
subjects are rather fuzzy.

WYNNE'S
"INFALLIBLE"
HUNTER METER
(PATENT.)

AUNT VITA AND HER TWIN, VIOLET

time. I couldn't believe you'd let that little bear trick you. Then that you clearly had—picking *bleuets!*—made me angry. As Balzac says— Oh. Ophelia, don't cry! Why are you crying? Isn't it better for you to hear this?''

I was surprised that I *was* crying. I reached up, touched a tear, snuffled, and tried to stop. It must be because I thought that Jean de Noël really liked me, I told myself. Now I knew he didn't—not in the way of real bears, who when they have deep feelings for each other are steadfast and sincere. I believed that Clarence

was telling the truth. He wasn't jealous; he wasn't making things up. For a moment I thought: I'm upset because Clarence isn't jealous! Then I thought: That's silly! and stopped crying. But it did seem as if Clarence thought *no* bear could possibly ever like me in a special way, just for myself, and that I was wrong for having thought that some bear did. This made me feel angry. I said, "*I know all about Jean de Noël, Clarence,*" and stood up and left the table, leaving Clarence looking very puzzled, scratching his head. I made my way back to the shop, tears and anger mixed in equal parts.

When Aunt Vita padded in at five o'clock, bearing pictures of herself and her twin sister, Violet, for the window, I asked her whether she would mind if I appeared in the window too. She said, "Why, I'd love the company, my dear!" This made me feel better. I like Aunt Vita, and from now on, for the month of September at least, I'll have a reason to spend all of my time in my dear shop.

SEPTEMBER 8   Aunt Vita and I were sharing a chocolate chess pie in the window as a snack this morning, talking over the intricacies of the making of chapeaux, when we saw a sharp shadow glide across the feathers surrounding our bottom paws. I clambered over photographs and tea cups and spotted the shadow and its owner—Mona Lisa—standing hesitantly near the door. I climbed out of the window and took her arm and led her in, tilting on her tall shoes. Although she wouldn't take a piece of chess pie Aunt Vita held out to her, when Ricky dusted off her favorite stool and

whispered solemnly, "We really missed you, Mona Lisa. Please don't stay away so long again," I saw her smile grow wider.

SEPTEMBER 13   Aunt Vita has as many interests as her nephew Dr. Churchill has. She raises dogs. She makes hats for all her neighbors in Kent, because, she says, "a head without a hat is an unattractive head, my dear." (I quickly put a feather on my head.) She takes photographs. Every afternoon, as the sun's rays lengthen and M. Ritz and Ricky Jaune begin to sweep the shop, she climbs down from the window, waves good-bye, and goes off on a picture-taking expedition. She has already made a lot of acquaintances in the neighborhood: *clochards*, and an ancient chimney sweep, even mice and crickets; and yesterday she came back with a photograph of *Popi*. It was a stop-action picture, taken with his paw raised, liturgical robes swirling, and a sly smile on his face as he called something out from the front of what looked like a wine cellar filled with bingo tables. "He was shouting winning bingo numbers," Aunt Vita said, "and he took an immediate liking to me, dear. He gave me my first card free and encouraged me to stay all evening—although I was a stranger to him. Now that was kind, wasn't it?" I am not sure, but I don't think so. Shall I tell this to Aunt Vita?

Waktool

"It is Written."

FREDDY AND EDWINA

AUNT VITA AND DR. CHURCHILL

SCHNUFFY IN KYOTO, JAPAN

SEPTEMBER 16   Schnuffy is on his way back home! I am very excited. He is sailing on another boat, the slow *Mimosa*. His card said to expect him by the middle of next month. We'll plan a party for him and will serve white rice and kumquats!

SEPTEMBER 20   Albert and Anemone came to meet the Churchills earlier this evening. The two of them could hardly contain their joy. They have received a "letter of comfort" from an English banker that allows them to draw a large amount from an account for their expenses every month. Both were wearing new ascots, patterned with tiny bees and honeysuckle blossoms. Albert said he thought the money must be a conciliatory gift from the royal family, and Dr. Churchill, peering at the banker's coat of arms, agreed. Anemone invited all of us to tea; but before they left, I saw her slip Aunt Vita a crisp pink bill, after which Aunt Vita whispered, "Thank you, dear. You know it's only until tomorrow," and I began to be alarmed. I imagine that it is for Popi.

SEPTEMBER 22   Zenobia came flying into the shop a little late this morning, short of breath, a scrap of paper clutched in her paw. "Look, Ophelia," she said, holding it out to me. It was a map of a tiny plot of ground she and Conrad rented for the bees to stay in for the winter. "It's very near to Montparnasse," she said. The pride of the plot, she pointed out, is a tupelo tree, from which Conrad ("Wearing gloves?" "Rubber gloves. Why?" "Oh, no reason") hung the hive himself. They plan to visit the bees together every Sunday, when the Opéra and the Bazaar des Bears are closed.

Do pop in for tea, you are always welcome any day at 4 o'clock   A&A

PRINCE ALBERT AND ANEMONE

embellished with family names and photographs of Freddie and Edwina. She whooped and scampered out the shop door, calling gaily, "See you later, dear!" and turned toward the English bank on the rue de Babylone. It was Saturday and the bank was closed, so I didn't follow her. But I mentioned the scroll to Dr. Churchill later in the day, as he and I were strolling, *tête-à-tête*, toward the Arc de Triomphe, and he exclaimed, "Good heavens! That sounds like our family deed!" He ran back to their hotel. It *was* their family deed: Aunt Vita admitted that Popi talked her into selling the "little Churchill family house" and winning a bingo fortune in its place. Dr. Churchill impounded the deed. Popi has been remanded to his little room at the Italian embassy, the paper says. M. Grandiose is smiling in the picture.

SEPTEMBER 28   "Heidi, do you remember Conrad's birthday party?"

"*Mais oui,* divine *duchesse au chocolat,*" she says.

"Do you remember any bears . . . well, flirting?"

"Uhm . . . well, Zenobia and Conrad seemed pretty smitten with each other."

"Yes. Isn't that nice? But any other bears? Any small, pale-toast, dapper, handsome bears, for instance?"

"Uh-oh! I hear Clafouti calling! Have to run, Ophelia! Nice to talk with you!"

The direct approach is not always the best approach. I wonder if Saint Bearnadelle said that.

SEPTEMBER 26   There is a picture in this morning's *Le Figaro* of Popi being led away in handcuffs by M. Grandiose. The story says he had been fixing bingo matches in the cellar of the church of St.-Etienne. Aunt Vita isn't in the picture—praise the Lord! I have been worried about her. Yesterday the postman brought her a large parchment scroll,

October

CONRAD

MONA LISA WITH PRINCE ALBERT, ANEMONE, AND M. RITZ

O C T O B E R

OCTOBER 2   Zenobia and I are sitting, stiff as boards, at our respective desks, watching the shadows of evening soften toward twilight. M. Ritz is on my lap, Ricky is standing like a sentry behind Zenobia's chair, Aunt Vita is keeping watch from the window, and Mona Lisa is pacing and tottering outside the door. We are waiting for Dr. Churchill and Conrad, who are walking slowly, arm in arm, toward the Bazaar des Bears—Dr. Churchill straight and stern, Conrad dressed in velvet gloves and carrying, like a convict with his ball, the crystal egg.

Conrad is the first into the shop. He is trembling from head to paw. Just as Dr. Churchill walks in behind him and pulls the curtained door to, Conrad turns a little and we see the egg. He is clutching it as though he wanted to make it part of his long trenchcoat, which, indeed, it seemed to be at first, except for its rosy glow. Dr. Churchill says austerely, "All right, Conrad. Tell everyone what has happened."

Conrad doesn't raise his eyes from the floor. He says slowly but loudly enough for all of us to hear, "*I* stole the crystal egg from the Bazaar des Bears. I also stole the honey, the tea, the tea service that was on the shelf, and the five enameled berry jars. I—I'm sorry." Then he looks at the crystal egg now as if he would dash it to the ground, puts his weight on one paw and then the other, and begins to cry.

I see Zenobia move from her desk chair as though to rise and run to Conrad, but her face is pale and she's been taken too much by surprise, I guess, because she falls back. "Why . . .?" she says. I kneel by her side and pat her. I want to say to Conrad, "How could you do this, you bad bear?" yet I want to go to him and comfort him as well. His eyes never leave the floor.

Dr. Churchill says, "Explain when and why you took these things, Conrad. Tell everyone here what you told me." Speaking to us, Dr. Churchill says in an aside, "I met Conrad in the foyer of his *pension de famille.* He was carrying the crystal egg in his arms when I encountered him—about to bring it back the way he did the berry jars, you see. I told him I thought it would be best to bring it openly, while you were here. Otherwise we might have recourse to Monsieur . . . Monsieur . . ."

"Monsieur Grandiose," Ricky says.

Conrad raises his face, tear-streaked, for just an instant and says, "No, Dr. Churchill! You didn't have to threaten me!" Then he lowers it again. "I wanted to bring it back," he says. "I was going to bring *everything* back, all by myself . . . except the tea and the honey, which I ate." Here he gives a little sob and says, "But—but—"

"But what, Conrad?" I say softly, my arm still around Zenobia's shoulders like a shawl.

"But I . . . I didn't . . . I didn't want Zenobia to know!" He drops the egg to the window ledge, where it *thunks* and gleams translucent in a ribbon of light coming from the street, and slumps next to it in a tangle, head in velvet gloves; but when the gloves touch the fur of his forehead, we see him start. He pulls them off and tosses them, crumpled, to the floor, whispering, *"Je renonce."*

Aunt Vita and I agree in whispers that it is time to take Zenobia home; she hasn't spoken but is trembling very hard. I wonder briefly whether she will be able to forgive Conrad. She is a generous bear, but this is a stinging disillusionment. We still don't know why he has taken these things from us, but it seems certain why he's brought them back, and we walk past him through the door M. Ritz holds open and into the street.

Later, when the bells of St.-Sulpice have struck eleven and Zenobia is safely tucked in bed, I've a long talk with Dr. Churchill, who comes alone to our rooms; he's sent Conrad to his rooms. He tells me he came to be in Conrad's pension that evening because he'd been "surveilling" Conrad all month long; unknown to us—ever since he had eliminated, one by one, the other suspects in the case. "Jean de Noël?" I ask. "Not in Paris during the commission of some of the crimes—I checked thoroughly," Dr. Churchill says. "In Deauville, he checked into a hotel on the beach with another bear when the berry jars were secreted back into the shop. In Monte Carlo last November. Never alone. Unshakable alibis." I clear my throat to ask, "Was it a female bear he was with in Deauville?" but Dr. Churchill, appearing uncomfortable and becoming brusque, pretends not to hear me. He says:

"Mona Lisa—*ahem!* Strange case, not a thief. Appears to have some longstanding connection with Conrad." He describes how Mona sometimes stands for hours outside Conrad's pension or behind the Opéra when he

is working there, and then will follow him—but only when he is wearing gloves. "That is what called *my* attention to Conrad's use of gloves, my dear," Dr. Churchill says. "I noticed them last April, of course, but they became suspicious later." So he followed Conrad too. Whenever Conrad put on gloves, Dr. Churchill noticed, he also adopted a furtive, disordered manner and tended to go where food and luxurious food-related items were. Late one afternoon, for instance, Conrad walked through a Right Bank gallery, Mona behind him and Dr. Churchill behind Mona. They each had watched him pocket a pre-Colombian carving of a groundnut. A few minutes later he retraced his steps and put it back. He did this with an air of longing, regret, and strained self-discipline. From that afternoon Dr. Churchill was pretty sure he'd found our burglar, and he continued to watch him in the hope of finding positive proof. Hence he and Mona were both concealed behind separate loquat trees in Conrad's lobby when Conrad emerged from his rooms with the crystal egg. Dr. Churchill apprehended him; Mona scurried off to forewarn us.

One more thing, Dr. Churchill says: When he and Conrad were walking together through the streets toward the shop, Conrad said ardently in answer to a reprimand by Dr. Churchill, "I've tried to stop! I've tried so hard!" A little mollified by this, Dr. Churchill said, "Then why do you do it, son?" Conrad said, "I—I've done it since I was a cub," and seemed to sink into a frightened reverie and would say no more.

"He has all the symptoms of an incurable

DR. CHURCHILL

SCHNUFFY

kleptomanic, Ophelia," Dr. Churchill says. "By Mona Lisa's request, I left him in her custody. But it might be best for all concerned to notify the *commissariat de police,* my dear."

"Oh, no, Dr. Churchill," I say, and suddenly I think that Clarence is just as smart as Dr. Churchhill and would have let him slip the egg back into the shop when we went out to dinner, without telling anybody else. I wished that Clarence were there to advise me then.

OCTOBER 4   M. Gris, the postman, enters the shop this morning as Aunt Vita and I are preparing to bring Zenobia tea and madeleines in her room, where we've kept her tucked in bed. He hands me a note from Mona Lisa, which asks me to meet her at her *meublé* at number 15 place d'Aligre at four o'clock tomorrow afternoon. I've never known before exactly where she lives.

OCTOBER 5   Clarence says, "Conrad? I can't believe my ears. I've grown so fond of the little fellow. I was half expecting our hard-bitten Zenobia to announce her engagement to him."

"This isn't funny, Clarence," I say. "Zenobia is still staying in her room. Yesterday she said to me, 'I always thought that I would die an early death.' Ricky's been attending to her bees."

"Zenobia doesn't mean it," Clarence says, picking up his suitcase from the salon floor. "I missed you," he says then, and kisses me on the cheek. "I'll go and see her."

Why do I feel happy? I dress to go to Mona Lisa's.

OCTOBER 6   Mona Lisa's room is in an old building on a quiet, dingy street in the market district that didn't promise much, and it took me by surprise. She opened her peeling wooden door into a room that was a trove of bright and sparkling things tucked away in every corner: There were painted ribbons and sashes from one-half inch to a foot wide; twenty-five-button gloves; silk flowers; bolts of moires, jacquards, and cashmere; old lace and tapestry; hand-painted silk velvet; and stacks of books on spinning, weaving, lacemaking, and wattling. Mona said, "Come in. Don't be surprised. My father made cloth, and my mother saved one piece of everything he made when his factory was closed down. I've brought you little scraps of it and other things I've found from time to time."

She showed me where to sit on a brocaded stool, wobbled herself to a chair, and sat down, explaining: "My father's factory was taken away from him in the war. My family was lost and scattered. We once were wealthy bears. Conrad—I met him on the streets many years ago, after I came by myself to Paris—was never wealthy. Let me talk about him first, Ophelia. He once told me he was a foundling cub, and when I first saw him he was living in a tiny bare room near the quai Voltaire and working his way through drama classes at the university. He was always angry and sometimes hungry; and he used to tell everyone he was rich, but he stole things—mostly food. He hated people to know that he was poor, except me, because I was poorer than he was. I don't think anyone ever loved him. Poor Conrad.

"When I saw him visiting your shop one day a year or so ago, I thought that maybe I should warn you that Conrad steals. But I couldn't. Maybe Conrad will really make friends, I thought. Maybe he'll learn he doesn't have to put on his costume gloves and take things to be happy. Then one day I saw him standing on a corner near the Bazaar, wearing fine leather gloves, with another pair of lace gloves in his paw. He thrust the lace gloves toward me as I walked by, saying, 'Take these. You need them too.' I tried to give them back, but Conrad ran away. I thought he was making me his accomplice in a crime, and I was frightened. I brought the gloves to you. Later, when I heard about the things that were missing from your shop, I couldn't understand it, even though I understood Conrad, because I knew he liked you, so I followed him. He talked about your partner all the time. I heard him telling a stagepaw at the Opéra once, 'She is true and generous and beautiful.' Perhaps he was afraid that if she found out how he grew up or the things he did, she wouldn't like him anymore; and he despaired. Perhaps he was testing you, and himself.

"I asked you to come here today to tell you about Conrad and about myself too. In some ways I'm the same as Conrad—solitary, dwelling in days gone by, but I don't want to be that way anymore. No one ever comes here. I thought we might be able to be friends."

"Won't you come to work for me in the Bazaar des Bears, Mona Lisa?" I said suddenly. You can be our buyer of lace and hats and cloth. You know more about those things than any of us! Won't you please?"

Mona Lisa's face was bright. She said, "Thank you," very softly. Then we agreed that she would start making her first appearance in the window, which was empty because Aunt Vita was packing to go home to Kent. I walked all the way back to the rue de Varenne, watching yellow leaves fall from the trees, wondering now and again at how little we bears sometimes know of one another (Conrad; Mona Lisa, whom I never even knew could talk that way; Jean de Noël) and contemplating how I might best tell Zenobia that in some strange way Conrad may have done what he did for her.

OCTOBER 13 Schnuffy returned last evening dressed in native robes, full of high spirits, with tales about the Orient and presents for us all. We put our arms around his skinny shoulders and all buzzed at once. A rice diet for six months! Zenobia has already learned to use the boxwood abacus that Schnuffy brought her; she's cheered up a little and is going over the September shop accounts in her room. Clarence is now standing before the mirror in the salon, calling out to me, "Do you really like this felt alpaca vest?" which Schnuffy says is a T'ai Chi master's vest. My gift is an intricate camphor chest with many little drawers and alcoves tucked inside the polished surface of a smooth, unbroken wooden cube, like a Chinese puzzle. This morning Schnuffy's sumi drawings are hanging on the furniture to dry, and his ink stone sits in the middle of the floor on a muslin sheet, surrounded by colorful spatters and smears.

November

CAMILLE WITH JEAN DE NOEL

N O V E M B E R

NOVEMBER 1   Camille has asked us to devote the November window to promoting *The Nutcracker Suite,* and so this morning Mona, Ricky, M. Ritz, and I cleaned out the window while Schnuffy brought in toe shoes, wands, and sized netting, which prudent Heidi has been keeping underneath all her beds since she took dancing lessons as a cub. We hung a facsimile of a stage curtain and then were just about to leave the shop for a festive cup of chocolate when we heard *Thump! Rattle! Crash!* and watched the curtain falling down on Schnuffy's furry head. Perhaps it wasn't sugar after all. Is Schnuffy doing Tai Chi in the window? He's told us he wants us all to learn.

NOVEMBER 3   The window is finished, and for the first two weeks of the month, before Camille's performances start, she is posing in her costume as well as in her photographs, which are scattered around her like a long, full skirt; and a lunchtime clutch of cubs and bears gathers before the shop each day, just like in front of Macy's Christmas windows, and they cheer when Camille dances a *paw seul.* M. Gris, who I think is enamored with her, delivers the mail three times a day, and hands our letters to Zenobia with his neat head turned at an angle to watch Camille balance on one paw.

Zenobia is back at work, but she is slow-pawed and meditative and treats the stock and her papers as if they were the ones that had suffered a blow and needed care. Still, her mood of despondency has been mixed with a lighter substance: Hope? On one of M. Gris's

visits earlier this week, he brought her a letter from Dr. Churchill, and Zenobia read part of it to me. "Such disorders as the one I believe Conrad suffers from are not incurable," Dr. Churchill wrote. "*Cf.,* the case of bears in Healy's *Roots and Fruits of Crime.* P.S. I took rough measurements of Conrad's head and can say with confidence that he was not born with a criminal streak." Aunt Vita added, in her shaky hand, "Come and visit us, my dear! I am knitting snow caps for you all!" Zenobia even chuckled a little bit at this—we have far too much style for snow caps!—before she went back to sit at her desk, abacus in hand, and look absentmindedly through her account books.

NOVEMBER 4   Jean de Noël was in the window talking with Camille this afternoon. He came through the door and bowed to me, but I pretended to be busy counting out little chocolate biscuits for our tea and not to see him, so he peered around the shop, as I see now that he *does* do—a darting movement with his eyes!—and climbed into the window when he thought I wasn't looking. My heart gave not a thump. I could hear Camille and him whispering together about the production—rose stage lights and the Sugar Plum Fairy chorus—through tea and on toward twilight, and I wasn't jealous—well, not until I looked out the window and saw the two of them winding down the sidewalk after closing time, paw in paw, with a last few yellow leaves falling about them from the *marronnier d'Inde* tree like snow. They looked so nice together, like two acting bears in starring roles,

OPHELIA

CAMILLE

CAMILLE'S BALLET SLIPPERS

JEAN DE NOEL

that I thought: What about me? This thought passed as M. Ritz squeaked at me and held out a tray with an aperitif and a nibble of cheese.

NOVEMBER 8   Mona Lisa is wonderful. Even Zenobia thinks so. She often talks now, and her smile is less timid, even when customers are here. She has many acquaintances from the street, and they all seem to have their sources too. Yesterday one of them brought a trunk packed with napthaed evening dresses from the attic of an old *hôtel* that had been condemned, and when we unbuckled the cinches, black beads from a Vionnet sheath winked at us. Beneath it was a pleated midnight-blue Fortuny dress with a pooling train.

CAMILLE

Dearest Ophelia
I live again! my paw de
deux has left me at last &
I am looking forward to re-
hearsals as much as the
performance. It is amazing
that ones life can take such
turns! I love you, Camille

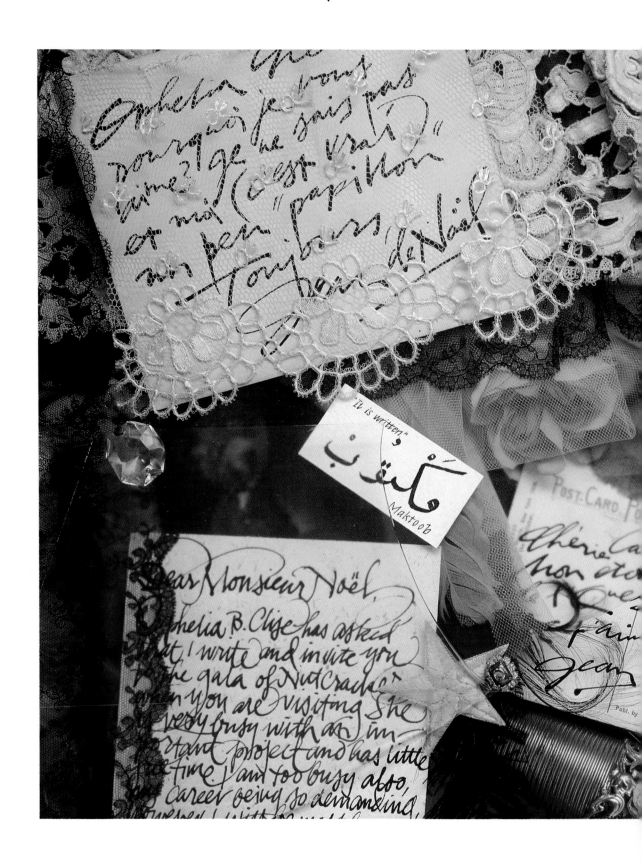

OPHELIA'S DESK FOR NOVEMBER

fat letter for Zenobia. As she took it from his paw and before she padded to her desk and then into the back room to read it, I recognized a quavering version of a schoolbook-perfect hand: Conrad's.

NOVEMBER 14   I am still in bed and the roofs are turning golden with pale noon sunshine. We were out at the ballet until almost morning. The reviews, which Heidi brought me on a tray with chocolate, are very good, and it seems that the production is a wild success. Everything *was* splendid, and everyone we knew was there. Albert and Anemone took a box and looked perfect and endearing in their new evening clothes. Clarence in a steely black tuxedo looked massive and imposing; on the other hand, Zenobia and I looked like elegant Edwardian maidens in trailing pale silk gowns. The palais de Chaillot was fuller than I remember its ever having been, and the weather was just warm enough to spend the intermission drinking Perrier-citron and eating Clarence's discovery of chocolate-covered pine nuts on the terrace, under the stars, from which we gazed out at the lighted splendor of the Champ-de-Mars and the Eiffel Tower. The *Suite* was beautifully danced and flawlessly paced—Camille's triumph. After the curtain

A Merry Christmas to thee and thine.

We hung eight dresses from strings around the shop, and today we sold them *all!*—I smuggled two from the trunk into the back room for Zenobia and me to wear to the ballet as a surprise.

NOVEMBER 12   On M. Gris's second visit to the shop this morning he brought a very

fell we applauded until Camille had taken her fourth bow, and then the whole audience rose as one and called out: "*Bravo!* Producer!" He was listed on the program only as Anonyme Modeste, or unknown one, and the audience wanted to know who he was. After a few minutes, I called out with them; I wanted to know too. Slowly a short, dapper bear in black evening dress made his way from the wings onto the stage, peering left and right about him. It was Jean de Noël! I should have known this, I told myself, from the way he seemed to know so much about the *Nutcracker* when he and Camille were whispering about it in the window. I didn't mind. But, when he and Camille bowed together and the audience began to cheer, Clarence took my paw in his and I felt even better.

NOVEMBER 21   Camille has been offered a permanent position as prima ballerina and artistic director of the Ballet de Paris, and several international stars have announced that they would like to come and dance with her. She stopped into the shop this morning to give us all a kiss. It is hard to say what in her new life makes her happiest, but Jean de Noël is now always by her side.

NOVEMBER 25   As a surprise, Mona Lisa and Schnuffy have designed a Christmas card for the Bazaar des Bears and had copies assembled from little scraps of lace and leftover ballet-school netting. The cards are very pretty, and we're busy addressing them to all our friends.

NOVEMBER 29   Zenobia is gone! Her note reads only: "Ophelia: I love Conrad. He asked me to marry him. We'll let you know where we have gone. Forgive him! Your Zenobia Onassis."

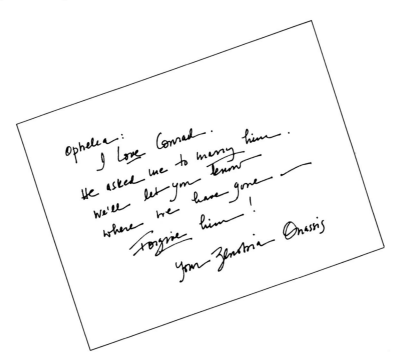

December

RICKY JAUNE, OPHELIA, ZENOBIA, AND M. RITZ

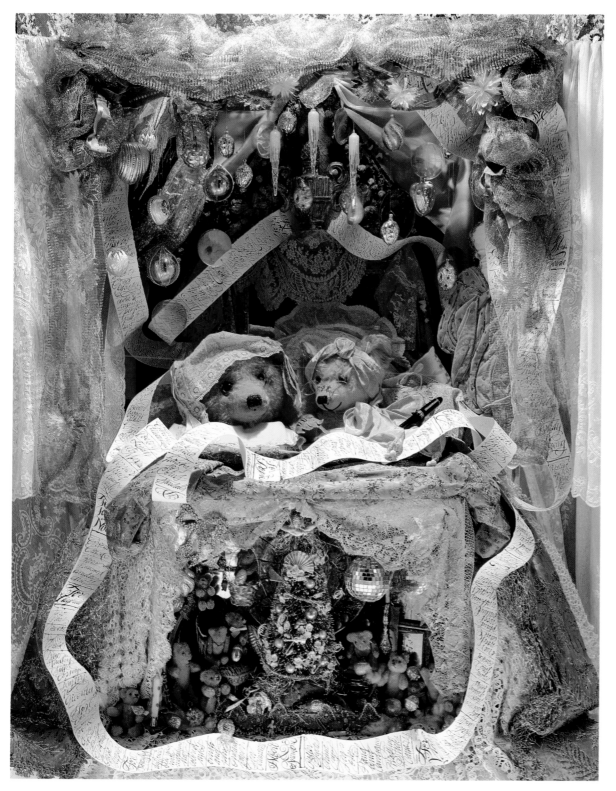

ZENOBIA AND OPHELIA WITH THE TEENY BEARS

D E C E M B E R

DECEMBER 1   I think that Clarence and I must be growing to be alike; our walks along the river almost always lead us to Bertillon's for cones filled with *glace aux fraises.* Without our saying anything to each other about it, even when the air is turning frosty in the steel-blue dusk of an early winter evening. This evening we walked across two bridges and as far as the brightly lit Right Bank streets, lined with shops already decorated for Noël. Pointing here and there with his paw, Clarence said that the shops must have taken their best ideas from the Bazaar des Bears. It is true that the windows are full of old dolls and doll clothes, toy soldiers, and faded tin wind-up toys tucked among the shoes and gowns and bracelets that are for sale, making them look like giants' clothes. We walked on, planning the final details of our own December window, which will re-create a cub's bedroom on a Christmas morning in another century. It will have the added attraction of allowing us a place to nap whenever we want to hide for a little while from the crush of Christmas shoppers.

Clarence is sentimental about Christmas. As we walked he told me stories about Noëls of his childhood: the sleighs and rocking horses, the steaming bowls of chocolate and *tartines beurrées.* He asked me, "Do you ever want cubs of your own, Ophelia?" and when I, with surprise, answered yes, he seemed quite pleased. I ascribed this to a circumstance I have elsewhere noticed: The best-hearted bears— and Clarence is good-hearted!—like to think of cubs at Christmastime. Clarence seemed more pleased than this accounted for, however; he clapped me on the back and forced his ice-cream cone on me, then clasped his paws together and began whistling a tune.

DECEMBER 2   This morning at breakfast Clarence said, "Let's have a Christmas party," and before he could put the next bite of waffle into his mouth, Ricky, Heidi, and Clafouti had pulled him from his seat and begun to plan it with him. Now we're slipping invitations into the remaining Christmas cards, and hoping once again for snow.

DECEMBER 8   I think I like this month's window best of all. We borrowed Zenobia's high old bed from the rue de Varenne and hung above it the silver canopy from mine, so it looks like a bed in a tower. This morning Mona Lisa arrived with five new street friends in her wake, brought to make ornaments for the Christmas window and the tree. Each one has a different skill: One sews, another prints with a tiny silkscreen, a third gold-leafs, a fourth beads and appliqués, and the fifth blows glass with a portable pipe he carries in his pocket. They have made twelve ornaments already, and they're the prettiest ones we have ever had. I hear them humming as they work in the back room.

There is music from the front of the shop. While I was puzzling over Zenobia's abandoned account book last night (so neat!), Clarence came in with a troupe of teeny dancing bears from the Cirque Médrano, who had temporarily lost their leader. They were sitting lined up on a park bench when Clarence, passing by, saw them. Knowing I was working late he brought them here, and they slept under the bed in the window. Today they are putting on a floor show from the pillows, with miniature banjos and guitars. M. Ritz didn't know what to make of them at first; he may have thought they were miniature cats, for he squeaked at them and feinted a sprint toward the front door. When they just stood and gazed at him as though they thought *he* might be a little cat, he looked to me and I introduced them to one another. Now he's assisting them on tambourine.

DECEMBER 15   Père Noël burst into the shop today, walked straight up to me, and said: "Have you been a good girl? Ho, ho, ho." This took me so much by surprise that I started to wonder whether I *had* been a good girl. I remember the time I hid Clarence's galoshes in a rainstorm and then a vague, discomfiting picture of Jean de Nöel flashed into my mind. Père Noël began to chortle, and then to laugh, and then to *shake* with laughter until his beard fell crosswise from his face and I recognized Clarence's chin. Soon everyone was laughing. Ricky insisted that we show Clarence off at the Café-Tabac, down the street, and so, with the worker bears from the back room and the dancing bears from the window, we all filed out. We must have made a fanciful picture, because two *agents des postes* bears on bicycles lifted their paws from their handlebars and waved as we passed by. Clarence gave each of the *garçons* at the café walnuts and an orange

and awarded the *patron* two lumps of coal for his bad food.

As we were leaving again, Clarence sidled up to me and said strangely, "Ophelia, I have something I've wanted to say to you for a long time. Now, I—"

"You what, Clarence?" I said. If this was to be bad news—Clarence getting married and running away from the Bazaar des Bears—I didn't want to hear it. I picked up my pace.

Clarence footslogged after, with a look mixed of whimsy and distress, and was fairly shouting, "I love—" when I walked into the blue canvas-covered chest of dear M. Gris, who had been walking down the street to meet us with a postcard extended in his paw. When he recovered his balance he said excitedly, although with a note of reproval in his voice, "It's from Zenobia." Clarence and Ricky rushed up as I took the little card, which had a picture on it of an old stone chapel in Calais, and read out: "Having a wonderful time. Recommend marriage to you all. Conrad almost cured. One week longer, Dr. Churchill says. Love, Madame Zenobia. P.S. Ricky: Please go to Montparnasse and feed the bees." Madame Zenobia! The card was postmarked Kent, England, and when we closely inspected the photograph on the front, we saw that two stick figures emerging from the oaken chapel doors, holding paws, had been drawn in the brown ink Conrad sometimes used to write his letters. We were all babbling together as we walked back to the shop, and so Clarence wasn't able to finish his sentence. . . .

. . . until later. He followed me around all day like a fly, from the shop front to the

OPHELIA'S DESK FOR DECEMBER

counter, where I was wrapping Christmas presents, to the back room to bring our industrious worker bears refreshments—even out to tea. But I evaded him. I kept Ricky with me every minute, and on my way to tea I ducked into M. Ritz's favorite little cheese shop and watched as Clarence hurried by. I have never seen Clarence so determined to say something to me! Finally he caught me. I was stepping out of Le Dilettante, checking left and right up the street, when a paw reached out from beside the door, clasped me by the shoulder and spun me round. "It's *you* I love," Clarence said loudly, his eyes shining down at me like topaz. "If you don't love me, please say so. If you do, please marry me." Then he did something he had never done before: He kissed me. He almost ruined it by saying through the kiss, "After all, you didn't care that much for Jean de Noël, did you?" but I kissed him hard, and this prevented him from talking.

Now I'm sitting in my boudoir. I've written to my parents in Alaska and now am planning what to write to Zenobia. She's the only other one I'll dare to tell. Clarence spent the evening making plans; he wrote down a January wedding menu; he said we should make up for Zenobia and Conrad's elopement by inviting everyone we know to a huge wedding, *including* Jean de Noël. Then he kissed me two more times and said, "We don't *have* to have a big wedding, you know. We could have a small wedding. We can have any kind of wedding you want, Ophelia. Let's elope." Later he said, "I *was* jealous. I was *very* jealous. You were right." Eventually I had to tickle him in the ribs to make him settle down.

Oh, Madame Zenobia, come home!

DECEMBER 18 Ricky has been locked in negotiations with M. Lenôtre's Pâtisserie for hours; the old bear says it's far too late now to begin ordering a bûche de Noël for Christmas Eve. We should have thought of that before. "But listen, it's for Ophelia B. Clise's Bazaar des Bears' Christmas party," Ricky says. "I don't care if it's for the Archangel Michael," Lenôtre shouts, so loudly I can hear him. "And you're invited!" Ricky screams, and there's dead silence on the phone; then a mild voice says, "And what time would you like it?"

DECEMBER 22 Schnuffy is making chocolate-chip-mint rice cakes. Heidi is mixing oranges with Grand Marnier. Ricky is dusting up a storm in the *salon*, and M. Ritz is trying to catch the flying particles in a little dustpan and sneezing. I am hanging Mona Lisa's friends' lovely ornaments on our tree. It is snowing.

DECEMBER 24 I stand in the doorway of our rooms in our *hôtel particulier*, poised with one paw out to greet our guests. There is a knock at the door. The count and countess enter calmly and demurely, kissing me on both cheeks. They move into the *salon*. No one is behind them; the apartment is as quiet as a cave. I turn to Clarence and say, "Where are our guests, do you suppose? Did Ricky forget to give the cards and invitations to Monsieur Gris?" when a shout rises up behind me, and turns into a roar. My parents are the first people I see. Maman! Papa! They rush to me and clasp me in their arms. Golda's high alto voice soars up behind us, and there is Moshe, by Golda's side. He calls. *"L'chaim!"* Brady Boeing throws a kiss into the air, and catches his paw on his eyepatch and skews it. Zenobia steps out of the crowd—Zenobia!—and puts one arm around my waist and one around my mother's waist and says, "Well, Ophelia, *two*—no, *three*—old married bears." I kiss her and start to cry. She pats my shoulder and says, "Now, now. There, there. Don't blame *me. I* didn't tell. Clarence did." I turn to Clarence and he's grinning. He shrugs and holds out his arms to me to dance. I go to him. We whirl through the crowd of all our friends as through an animated forest. The snow contiues to fall through the lights outside. Zenobia and Conrad glide onto the floor to join us, and our friends call, *"Changez vos partenaires!"* We change partners. I think of all that's happened in this year: true loves, false loves, a celebration of fifty years of happy marriage, new friends, old friends, trips, quarrels; reunions, two new business partners for the Bazaar des Bears (for it's just occurred to me, seeing Ricky handing out champagne, that he has grown up and must also become our partner), and, yes, why not another shop? I watch Conrad as we dance, looking sober and ashamed but upright too, for the first time having the unnameable air of a bear who is well loved; and the others—Dr. Churchill and good old Vita, who must have traveled with Zenobia and Conrad over the Channel; Heidi, Clafouti, M. Dilettante, Albert and Anemone, Marcello, Popi! M. Grandiose! M. Gris, Camille, and Jean de Noël, who just now is looking longingly at *me;* Mona Lisa and her

friends; Ricky Jaune and M. Ritz; and dear, darling Schnuffy. Before they all begin to dance, I whisper to Conrad, "Welcome home. I love you too," and then I kiss him and move on to dance with Clarence, my true love.

DECEMBER 30   Zenobia and I are lying snuggled together in the window bed. We stretch and yawn. She says to me, in a languid, snoozy voice, "I'm very happy." I say to her, "I'm happy too." I pause for a minute and then I say, "You know, I think Saint Bearnadelle might have a phrase for us: "More *is* sometimes enough," and we drift off to sleep.

CLARENCE

OPHELIA

A C K N O W L E D G M E N T S

I would like to thank the following people for making *Ophelia's World* possible:

SEATTLE—Marsha and Michael Burns for the many hours of work and creative expertise they cheerfully and generously gave; Richard Holmes Nelson for devising the shop window; Tim Girvin who also created and styled the cards, handwritings, sumi drawings, invitations, and paper ephemera that make up Ophelia's collection of papers; Tina Hoggett and the Day Moon Press for the letterpress work; Tom McMackin who so generously gave up his time to prepare and help Ophelia's original presentation in New York; Ed Marquand for his moral support from the very beginning, especially the first days in Manhattan; Philip Archibald and Marjan Willemsen of Tim Girvin Design, Inc. who worked so diligently on this project; Louis Nawrot, my attorney, who is always there when we need him; Richard Tyler Nelson for ironing Ophelia's ruffles and packing her suitcases; Alf and Shirley Collins and their computer, Madeleine, who always have supported me in any and all of my efforts; François Kissel and Jean-Paul Kissel for their patience with Ophelia's "French" and with refining her palate; Camille McLean who accompanied Ophelia and Clarence on their first journey to Paris; Bruce Guenther, curator of Seattle Art Museum's Contemporary Collection for developing Heidi and Clafouti's art appreciation; D. Taylor Davenport the Dilettante, for creating Zenobia's special chocolate recipes; Susanna Pinyuh, Claire Meisel, and Marianne Meisel for their faith and support of Ophelia; Diane Millican, Susan Ohlson-Elo, Beverly McDevitt, Sheri Sayre, and Collins Jones for their loyal patronage that helped us through last winter; Robert Shields who first discovered Ophelia; Leroy and Joie Soper who always had the time to encourage us; John Clise who loved Ophelia from the beginning, and all the wonderful customers of my shop, Bazaar des Bears®.

NEW YORK—Laura Besserman for steering me to Barbara Burn, who generously introduced me to Carol Southern at Clarkson N. Potter who believed in Ophelia at first sight; Carol Leslie for her patience and her endless support; Ruth Andrews for her belief; Dennis Hadley who knew four years ago the bears were "it"; Oscar Dystel for his time and interest in Ophelia's welfare; Carolyn Hart and Michael Fragnito and everyone at Clarkson N. Potter who worked so steadily to keep us on track; Gael Towey Dillon for working so well with Tim Girvin Design, Inc. on the design; Anne Heller who knew just the right thing to say; Baron von Hütter for his continuing interest.

PARIS—Serena Talfargio and Michele Loyer, "always there" when we lived there and when we return; Thérèse Dussaut and Claude Lemaréchal for helping Ophelia with her excess baggage and various other problems; the pastry shops of Gaston Lenôtre, and, of course, that most beautiful of cities, Paris.

MONTE CARLO—Nathalie Laurent-Hill, George Hill, and Jean de Noël for sharing this particular personality.

GIENGEN (BRENZ)—Herr Doctor Herbert Zimmermann, Herr Roland Zeller, Herr Jörg Junginger, and Margarete Steiff GmbH for their interest, faith, and expertise.

To the above and to all my friends who fell under the spell of Ophelia I offer my sincerest appreciation for all your patience, help, and humor in helping me make Ophelia come to life.

Michele Durkson Clise